D1459620

# Bird Girl

*and the* Man *who* Followed *the* Sun

# Bird Girl

## and the Man who Followed the Sun

An Athabaskan Indian Legend from Alaska

# By Velma Wallis

## Illustrations by Jim Grant

Foreword by William L. "Willie" Hensley

HarperPerennial

*A Division of* HarperCollins*Publishers*

*Also by Velma Wallis*

Two Old Women

Gwich'in language consultant: Jim Kari

This book was originally published in 1996 by Epicenter Press. It is here reprinted by arrangement with Epicenter Press.

First HarperPerennial edition published 1997.

*Designed by Newman Design/Illustration*

Library of Congress Cataloging-in-Publication Data

Wallis, Velma.
    Bird Girl and the man who followed the sun : an Athabaskan legend from Alaska / by Velma Harris ; illustrations by Jim Grant ; foreword by William L. "Willie" Hensley. — 1st ed.
        p.   cm.
    Originally published: Fairbanks : Epicenter Press, c1996.
    ISBN 0-06-097728-0
    1. Athabaskan Indians—Folklore. 2. Legends—Alaska. I. Title.
E99.A86W35    1997
398.2'089'972—dc21                                                    97-19793

00 01 RRD 10 9 8 7 6

*This book is dedicated to all tribes of the globe.*
*We are all different individually, in groups,*
*and as nations, yet we must rise above*
*indoctrinations of hate and evil, and struggle*
*together as one tribe for what is good.*
*Historically, we have all suffered and endured.*
*May we have the trust to face our future.*

*Velma Wallis*

# Table of Contents

# Foreword

As an Inupiaq, I was at first distressed to see my people portrayed as the villains in the Athabaskan legends retold in *Bird Girl and the Man Who Followed the Sun*. Among my earliest memories of growing up along Alaska's Arctic Coast were stories of warfare between the Inupiat and the Athabaskans of the Interior. The two peoples shared a common border for millennia, and it was understandable that clashes occurred over hunting territory.

Stories told to us, however, portrayed the Athabaskans as stealthy and untrustworthy. When dealing with them, one had to be very careful.

In *Bird Girl*, Velma Wallis has drawn on Athabaskan legends to create a portrayal of lives in ancient Alaska that rings true from the perspective of her culture. It is a fascinating description of life at a time when rules and tradition, strength and knowledge, obligation and duty were critical to survival against the arctic elements. In those values the two cultures held much in common.

The main characters in the story, Daagoo and Bird Girl, come into conflict with those values. They experience the difficulties that individuals from all cultures face when their ideas and strong wills threaten the survival and solidarity of the group.

Despite the conflicts, some aspects of Inupiat-Athabaskan relations in ancient times were positive: extensive trade, alliances, intermarriages, and the sharing of technology. In modern times, it has been remarkable to see the cooperation between the Inupiat and the Athabaskans as they have fought a common fight for their ancestral territory. There is a unity of purpose as both groups work to rekindle their languages and traditional ways. For both cultures, the enemy today is the fading of the spirit, the distractions of modern life, the confusion of identity, and the loss of language.

These legends respond to such problems with a message of hope. Through all the trials and sorrows in their lives, Daagoo and Bird Girl have the courage to act on their hopes and dreams, to follow their own hearts and minds, never losing their ability to trust in the future.

Iġġiaġruk (William L. Hensley)

*William L. "Willie" Hensley, a prominent Inupiaq leader, co-founded the Alaska Federation of Natives, helping to unify Alaska's Native peoples.*

# Acknowledgments

I would like to thank Lael Morgan for helping me write this story. Without you, this book would not have emerged. Your no-nonsense "You can do it!" was exactly what kept me writing. Thank you, teacher.

Thank you to my mother for loving my children while I worked. Thank you again for giving me the two legends. Without you I would not have the desire to tell stories.

Thank you to Barry, my brother, my mentor, my pal, my greatest critic, and my equal in dreams for better things yet to come.

Thank you to Kent Sturgis, Christine Ummel, and Elizabeth Wales for taking me seriously even when I had lost faith in myself. Thank you a thousandfold to Christine Ummel for doing an excellent job fine-tuning the manuscript and for being tactful, gentle, and inspiring all the way. Your job is not easy. I honor you and your talent as an editor, for without editors there would be no good writing.

Thank you to Linda Wells and the Rural Education Center in Fort Yukon for the use of books, paper, and a computer when I needed it most.

Thank you to Judy Erick of Venetie once more for helping me with the written Gwich'in language.

And last but never, never least, Jim Grant, thank you for your illustrations, for without them my stories could never truly come to life.

God bless you all.
Mahsi'

Velma Wallis

# CHAPTER 1
## Two rebels

I n ancient times, in a land where the sun shone day and night in summer, then disappeared for much of the deathly cold winter, lived the Gwich'in. These Indians inhabited the flatlands surrounding the mighty river they called the Yuukon, south of the long stretch of mountains that spread from one end of the country to the other. To the north, beyond these peaks, along the coast of the northern sea, lived the Ch'eekwaii, the Eskimos who were their enemies.

Both peoples hunted the caribou that migrated in great herds across the vast landscape, every year traveling through the mountains from their wintering place to their calving grounds along the coast. Sometimes, in following these animals, the Ch'eekwaii and the Gwich'in crossed into one another's hunting grounds, violating boundaries they had been taught to respect. Eventually repeated trespassing and bloody reprisals created hatred between the two peoples.

In these times, in different bands of the Gwich'in, lived two Indian children, a boy and a girl, two rebels who went beyond the ordinary.

The boy was a handsome child, his long black hair braided around a face softened by youth. Except for his average height and lean, muscular body, he had little in common with his peers. Gwich'in boys were taught to enjoy hunting and competition, for they would be the strength of their people when they became men. Yet this boy was not interested in hunting, wrestling, or running games. He was a loner.

He was named Daagoo, in honor of a bird, the ptarmigan. The Gwich'in people revered the animals that roamed the land, and they wanted their children to emulate the strength and skills of the animals they admired, such as the ptarmigan. To help their children

become surefooted like the bird, many parents wove porcupine quills, naturally dyed with plants, into patterns of small ptarmigan feet on their children's moccasins.

Daagoo's parents went one step further by giving their son a name that meant ptarmigan. In time the boy became not only sure on foot, but as flighty as the bird itself, always running off to explore the lakes, sloughs, creeks, and rivers scattered throughout the flatlands.

When in camp, the curious boy spent his time asking many troublesome questions. One particular question brought amusement to the faces of many elders. Daagoo wanted to know what happened to the sun in winter, when it seemed to retreat into the south, rising less high in the sky each day until it disappeared below the horizon.

To satisfy the child, the elders told him about the Land of the Sun, a warm country to the south where the sun shone all year long. It was said that a group of

Gwich'in people had journeyed there many years ago. Some of them reached the Land of the Sun, while others turned back, afraid of entering unknown territory.

One elderly man said that his great-grandfather had been one of those who returned to the north. The elder described the ancient route to the Land of the Sun, passed on to him by his great-grandfather, and drew a map for little Ptarmigan in the dirt. Delighted, Daagoo copied the map onto a piece of tanned moose skin that his mother had given to him.

When Daagoo questioned other adults about this fabled land, or showed them his map, often they only frowned at him, for most people did not take such legends seriously. But Daagoo had complete faith in the legend. One day, the small boy vowed to himself, he would find the Land of the Sun.

Many miles from the places where Daagoo's band camped, there roamed another Gwich'in band, in which there lived a young girl. She was named Jutthunvaa' after the jewelry she wore. Ever since Jutthunvaa' was an infant, her mother, Na' Zhuu, had made jewelry for her, fashioning beads from the shin bone of the moose, dyeing them, and stringing them together into necklaces and bracelets to ornament her only daughter.

Despite all Na' Zhuu's efforts to make her daughter look beautiful and feminine, Jutthunvaa' was more influenced by her father and three older brothers. Her father, Zhoh, trained his children to make and use their own weapons. All Gwich'in men were expected to give such training to their sons, but no one was expected to train a daughter this way. In these times boys were trained to hunt and scout for animals, while girls were taught to cook, raise children, tan skins, sew, and gather edible plants and medicinal herbs. But Zhoh was proud of his daughter's interest in the things that he and his sons did, so he encouraged her to learn how to run and hunt.

The young girl was an eager student. She even learned to imitate perfectly the calls of the birds that flew through the flatlands — a skill which hunters prized highly, for they used birdcalls to signal to one another without frightening away the animals nearby. In time Na' Zhuu stopped trying to teach Jutthunvaa' how to cook and sew, surrendering her daughter to be trained by the men of the family. She no longer protested when Zhoh and his sons called Jutthunvaa' by their nickname for her, Bird Girl.

As the years passed, the daughter of Zhoh and

Na' Zhuu grew into a beautiful young woman. Bird Girl became a skilled hunter, able to run long distances and swim the swiftest rivers. She raced and wrestled with the boys in the camp, often beating them at their games. Her family watched her grow strong and skillful, feeling pride and admiration for the girl. Yet other members of the band began to frown.

In the camp where Daagoo lived, the men also frowned. They were losing patience with this boy who was always wandering away, exploring, instead of hunting or scouting for animals. His lack of interest showed blatant disrespect. Daagoo's father, Ch'izhin Choo, bore most of the men's criticism.

"He is your son and your responsibility," he was told.

Ch'izhin Choo had no answer to their complaints. He admitted that he and his wife had allowed their son to have his own way too long. Now that Daagoo was becoming a man, Ch'izhin Choo knew it would be hard to change him.

Daagoo did not mean to be a bad son. He loved his parents and tried to please them. Sometimes he hunted small animals, such as porcupines or ground squirrels, which were Gwich'in delicacies, and gave them to his mother as gifts.

Still, there was a part of Daagoo that he could not deny. He had an insatiable wanderlust. Often he worried his parents by roaming the land and not returning for days.

One evening, when Daagoo returned from a long walk, his father was waiting for him. With the criticism of the other men weighing heavily on his mind, Ch'izhin Choo began to question his son about his behavior.

Daagoo answered eagerly. "Father, I am curious about this land and beyond. I wonder about those mountains over there." He pointed to the distant peaks. "I wonder about the places we have never been. We travel the same paths to each campsite every year. We never stray from our course, and I look at the faraway mountains and wonder what is on the other side. Are you curious about things like that, too?"

"Son, if I sit and wonder about those mountains, will it bring us meat to eat?" Ch'izhin Choo asked his son earnestly. "Will it warm us on a cold winter night? If our people visited the mountains, it would cost many lives, for we would waste precious time when we could be hunting and gathering food for the winter. People would freeze and starve as a result of foolish curiosity."

Daagoo only half-listened. "Father, you do not even wonder about the sun?" he asked, disbelieving. "About where it goes at night and during those long winters when we struggle to survive the deep snow and cold? The elders have spoken about the Land of the Sun, a warm country where the sun shines all the time. We should follow the sun instead of suffering another cold winter here."

Ch'izhin Choo lost all patience, shaking his head in exasperation. Nothing he said had made an impact on his son.

"Even I look at the mountains and wonder what lies beyond, but Son, we have to keep our minds on what is important. Our survival! Nothing else can be important."

Ch'izhin Choo sighed tiredly, for he knew that convincing his son to change would not be as easy as the other men believed it would be. Daagoo dreamed of one day following the sun. It was this impossible dream that Ch'izhin Choo meant to destroy if he could, for he wanted his son to do what was right, to help keep his people alive by hunting for animals.

Not long after that, the band's chief and the other men in the council approached Ch'izhin Choo.

"We can no longer tolerate your son's behavior," one hunter said. "What if our lives depended on that boy? We would soon be dead. He does not even hunt!"

Stung by the challenge, Ch'izhin Choo was quick to defend Daagoo. "I have taught my son all there is to know about hunting. If you or the people are ever in need, he could save your life and the lives of everyone else in this camp!"

"Enough!" the chief said, holding up his hands to quiet the two men, who stood facing one another with clenched fists. "Arguing will not solve this problem. We must talk sensibly."

He turned to Ch'izhin Choo and said, "You will talk to your son. Tell him that we will no longer allow his disobedience. We all know what happens when people refuse to follow our rules."

Daagoo's father could do nothing but nod his head in agreement. The Gwich'in had lived in the flatlands for thousands of years and had established strict rules. For the band to survive, each member had to fulfill his or her duties without question. Obedience was enforced with punishment; people could be banished from the band for refusal to comply with its age-old customs. It was understood that, besides the animals and the land itself, the Gwich'in people needed each other for survival. They knew the importance of obedience and the terrible consequences of foolish rebellion.

## CHAPTER 2
## A meeting by the river

*B*efore Ch'izhin Choo could talk to his son, Daagoo left on another journey across the flatlands. There were so many places he wanted to explore. He especially liked to climb the hills farther north. Then he could look up to see the mountains far away, or look back to see the flatlands spread out for hundreds of miles, with the wide Yuukon River slicing through the country.

Today he found himself walking alongside that great river. In summer the biggest of all fish, the salmon, wrestled their way through its currents, upriver to where they were trapped by the Gwich'in and hung on willow racks to dry. The Yuukon had sustained the lives of the Gwich'in for as long as they could remember.

Daagoo followed an unfamiliar path, which was how he usually explored. It was the thrill of not knowing where a trail led that kept him going. Sometimes he traveled well-worn paths on the banks of the rivers and sloughs, only to have his way suddenly blocked by thickets or willow branches; these paths had been made by beavers or rabbits, who could easily crawl under such obstacles. He also discovered trails created by women, leading to bushes of berries.

Once, on a spring afternoon when the day was turning dark blue toward dusk, he had seen a rabbit and a fox bolt out of the willows, seeming to almost fly across his path as the predator pursued its prey. Daagoo could only marvel at the spectacle, wondering if any other humans ever witnessed such sights. At other times, his heart raced in fear as he worried about encountering some of the talking trickster animals described in his mother's stories.

During this particular walk, as Daagoo thought about all these things, he suddenly had a feeling that he was not alone, and he looked up to see a young woman. Before he could hide, she turned toward him. For a moment the two could only stare at each other.

From their earliest years, Gwich'in children were taught to fear strangers. Their parents frightened them by telling them that, if they made too much noise, the Ch'eekwaii would come from the north and steal them. Although this was intended only to keep the children quiet in case an animal was nearby, the stories filled the children's imaginations with terrifying images of the enemies they had never seen.

Now Daagoo relaxed a little when he saw that the girl wore a dress hung with pointed fringes in the Gwich'in style. His eyes took in the many-colored bone necklaces and bracelets that she wore, and the bow and arrows that she carried. This made him curious — it was strange to see a girl wearing jewelry and carrying weapons. Daagoo heard himself ask, "What are you doing here by yourself?"

The girl smiled in relief, understanding his words. "I am hunting," she answered simply.

Daagoo's brow lifted in surprise. During all the time that he spent exploring, he had never met another human, much less a girl hunting alone. He did not know how to react to this strange girl who blocked

his path. She did not move either and returned his stare.

"What is your name?" she asked finally.

He told her.

"I am Bird Girl," she said, although he had not asked her name. When Daagoo did not say anything, she asked, "What are you doing here?"

Daagoo paused as he tried to think of some way to explain. People who lived only for survival never understood why he spent precious time exploring.

"I am just walking," he mumbled.

Bird Girl's eyes lit with curiosity. She had never heard of someone just walking, and she wanted to know more.

Instead it was Daagoo who asked the next question. "Are your people nearby?"

He felt his face flush at her direct look. She was not like the women he knew. Normally, a woman would be afraid to look into the eyes of a man, especially those of a stranger. Yet she looked at him with curiosity and, instead of waiting for him, she spoke first.

"I am hunting on my own. My people are back in their camp," Bird Girl answered. She could tell that he was not like the other boys. The young men in her band treated her with anger and contempt, resenting the times when Bird Girl had fought with them and won. She knew they felt threatened by her strength and aggressive manner, but Daagoo did not seem intimidated. Still, she did not understand what he meant when he said he was simply walking. "Are you hunting, too?" she asked.

Daagoo decided not to give her a complete answer, for many times he angered people when he tried to explain about his exploring.

"I do not hunt very much. I am scouting," he told her instead.

Bird Girl sensed that this boy was not telling her everything, but she stopped asking him questions because his face had become hard like a mask.

The two young people stood on the banks of the mighty river that flowed below them. They stared out at the warm summer day that would shortly slip into the coolness of fall.

Finally Daagoo said, "I have to go." He wanted to continue his walk. This girl interested him, but restlessness urged him forward.

The two bid each other farewell. When Daagoo was some distance down the path, he looked back and found Bird Girl staring at him. Quickly he turned his head and walked away faster.

Bird Girl smiled and shook her head. He was a strange one. Sometimes unusual events interrupted the daily monotony of the struggle to survive. This chance meeting was something she would remember.

## CHAPTER 3
## The chief's decision

Bird Girl's father, Zhoh, stood in the darkening evening, looking up at a tiny speck of light in the center of the sky. When this small star appeared at this time of year, it meant summer was over. Now was the time to start planning for the winter again. He turned to go back into the skin tent where his wife sat. They both waited for Bird Girl, to tell her the news together.

"Is she here yet?" Na' Zhuu asked as her husband came into the shelter. He shook his head.

Zhoh heaved a deep sigh. He knew disciplining his daughter sounded like an easy thing to do, but it was not. Bird Girl was between the stages of being a child and a woman. She could be as docile as a fish swimming quietly beneath the waters, but at times her eyes would rage as rebelliously as those of an old

bear with many wounds in its body. Zhoh shuddered. He wondered where he would find the courage to tell his daughter about this decision.

Zhoh thought back to the days before this trouble began. He and his wife loved their daughter and had allowed her to run and hunt, instead of forcing her to concentrate on learning the skills of a Gwich'in woman.

No one objected at first. Like her brothers, Bird Girl began hunting, bringing in meat for her family and for other people who could not provide for themselves. Zhoh recalled his pride in the skills he and his sons had taught the girl. She could run long distances without tiring, leap over fallen trees, and hunt many kinds of animals. But what made Zhoh most proud was that Bird Girl could do all of this better than the young men in the band, including her own brothers. This reflected well on his teaching skills.

Not until today, when the other men had come to him with their complaint, did Zhoh realize his mistake. Despite the fact that Bird Girl brought back meat for her family, some of the men did not approve. They thought she should be married. A small group of men had gathered together to bring this to the attention of their leader.

The chief was a man who sought only to keep the peace, to help his people work together for their survival. He had no opinion about Bird Girl. He saw no harm in her being a hunter, but he saw no reason why she should not be married, either. Any man would be glad to have her now, and later she would be considered too old to marry. If everyone thought she should be married, then he would do his duty and make it happen.

With all the other men behind him, the chief stood before Zhoh and said in an indifferent voice, "Your daughter is old enough to be married. It is long past the day when she should have been matched with a man. We want you to choose a man for her."

Zhoh remained silent. He suspected that the men had resented his daughter for a long time. She was aggressive, always asking questions and looking directly at the men — unlike the other women, who listened quietly and obeyed the men without challenging their authority.

Zhoh wanted to defend his daughter and tell them she needed more time to accept the idea of marriage, but he could not argue with his fellow hunters. He knew that he was the one to blame. He had known the strict rules that his people had followed for generations, the traditions that kept everything in balance. Yet he had willfully indulged his daughter, breaking one rule that was never to be broken. He had taken over his wife's responsibility and trained his daughter himself. Now Bird Girl would pay the price for his mistake.

Late in the evening, Bird Girl's parents heard her moving about outside their shelter. She had brought home some porcupines and ducks, and was setting them by the campfire where her mother would cook them the next day.

As she was about to walk away, she heard her father's muffled voice from within the shelter. "Come inside," he ordered quietly.

Bird Girl was surprised, for it had been a long time since she had been asked into her parents' shelter. She stepped lightly into the tent, a willow frame covered by untanned caribou skins. There she found her parents sitting solemnly around their hearth, the embers beaming softly.

"Yes?" she said. Her questioning eyes belied the soft tone of her voice.

"Sit down," her father said.

Bird Girl sat cross-legged and looked at her parents. Her mother avoided her eyes, and her father's voice was strained. Something was wrong.

"What is it?" she asked.

Zhoh was a brave hunter, admired for his hunting skills and strength. The other men respected his tremendous courage in the most dangerous situations, but Zhoh knew they would mock him if they saw him now, for he could not summon the courage to speak to his daughter.

Na' Zhuu sensed her husband's reluctance and nudged him sharply. Zhoh spoke quickly, determined not to embellish his words. His daughter needed to hear the truth.

"The chief wants you to marry. He says that we can no longer wait. You know there can be serious punishment for those who do not obey his instructions," he told Bird Girl, who listened in stunned silence. "Tomorrow, when you are ready, we will find you a man."

At first Bird Girl reacted only with a blink of her eyes. She could not believe what she had heard, but she knew from her parents' seriousness that her father spoke the truth. She felt resistance building inside her.

"But, Father," she protested, "can't we wait until I am ready for marriage? I need more time!"

Bird Girl was aware that some of the people resented her. Often they had hurt her feelings, the girls teasing her, the boys treating her as if she were a strange animal, or the older men acting as if she had wronged them somehow. She always ran to her father for solace and understanding. Many times, Zhoh had assured his daughter that they would accept her one day.

Now he was not so blinded by love for his child. He realized she would never be accepted by her people until she learned to follow their rules.

"No, my daughter," he said. "Tomorrow we will do this together. We must obey, for our leader will have it no other way." His heart ached at the devastated look on his daughter's face.

Bird Girl said nothing. Even as Zhoh spoke, she knew she could not obey him. She could not marry a man she did not want; she could not have children now. She had known freedom, unlike the other women. Now the same person who had allowed her this freedom was trying to take it away. Bird Girl knew the traditions her people lived by, but she could not accept this one. She had been free too long.

Knowing anything she could say would provoke an argument, she remained silent as her mind raced with many thoughts, all looking for a way out of this trap. Her father knew her well, so she was careful not to show her emotions. Instead, she nodded her head submissively.

Zhoh was filled with doubt. He had seen the rebellion in his daughter's eyes for a moment, but when Bird Girl looked up at him again, Zhoh saw only deep sadness in her face. He relaxed, thinking she had decided to obey. Zhoh heard his wife let out a relieved sigh as Bird Girl stood up.

"We will see you in the morning, Jutthunvaa'," Na' Zhuu said softly. She wanted somehow to convey to her daughter that all would be well. Bird Girl nodded her head and left the tent.

Zhoh and his wife looked at each other. They had expected their daughter to throw a tantrum. Instead, she had hardly protested.

"She is very tired," Na' Zhuu said, trying to make sense of her daughter's behavior. They worried that after a night of rest and a good meal, Bird Girl would fight back with all her strength.

## CHAPTER 4
## An obedient son

*After saying goodbye to Bird Girl, Daagoo continued walking along the trail and discovered that it extended farther along the banks of the Yuukon than he had imagined. He walked for hours before deciding that he had gone far enough and heading home.*

*Back at the camp, Daagoo's parents were waiting, worried, for he had not told them he would be gone so long. His father was determined to hold his temper. He planned to tell Daagoo, as gently as he* could, that grown men were expected to act with responsibility and contribute to the band. But when Ch'izhin Choo saw Daagoo strolling into the camp with a carefree smile on his face, he became angry.

"How could you worry us like that?" Ch'izhin Choo exploded. "Have you no feelings? Your mother has been imagining all kinds of things happening to you!"

Daagoo, surprised by his father's outburst, tried to explain, but his father went on.

"If you continue acting like this, you will no longer be part of this family," he said.

Daagoo stared in disbelief. His parents had always allowed him to explore. Why this sudden change?

"Father, you cannot mean that," Daagoo managed at last.

"I mean what I say, Son. If you do not change your ways, I will have nothing to do with you." Ch'izhin Choo knew his words sounded harsh, but he was determined to change his son's behavior so that harmony could be restored to the band.

Daagoo turned to his mother for support, but she refused to look at him.

"Starting now, you will take part in all hunting and scouting, or you will be left on your own," Ch'izhin

Choo said. His voice softened as he saw the deflated look on Daagoo's face. "You must start acting like a true Gwich'in. Hunt and take care of your family. We need another hunter."

"Father, I realize that I have not done my share," Daagoo admitted. "If I do what you want, will you allow me to explore in my free time? I can do both."

Ch'izhin Choo eyed Daagoo carefully, for he had expected that his son would try to find a way out of this. "In time, Son, if you prove to be a good hunter," he answered evenly.

Silent resentment burned inside Daagoo at the thought of not being allowed to explore. He considered leaving the camp to live by himself, but he knew that he was not ready to survive on his own. Perhaps that time would come later. For now, he nodded his head in surrender.

It did not take long for Daagoo to conform to the ways of his people. Using the skills that his father had taught him, he hunted porcupines, rabbits, grouse, and ducks. All the people noticed the change in the young man. The other hunters nodded their heads in approval. They felt they had been right to persuade Ch'izhin Choo to correct his son, for Daagoo was proving to be a good hunter.

Daagoo saw that the band's attitude toward him had changed. "I could be a piece of wood for all they care," he thought angrily. "When I do what my heart desires, they reject me and threaten me. They only accept me when I do what they want."

One evening as the men prepared for a caribou hunt the next day, Daagoo sat at his mother's campfire, looking around the camp. The band would stay there for most of the winter, until the caribou moved on. Daagoo took in the sights, sounds, and smells of this familiar place. The air was filled with the scent of recent rain, which mingled pleasantly with that of the ground, trees, and smoke. Children laughed, and their parents could be heard hushing them in case animals were nearby.

Although this way of life was familiar and comfortable, Daagoo wanted more. He felt certain that if he stayed with the band, never leaving to follow his dreams, his spirit would slowly die.

A few feet away, Daagoo's mother, Shreenyaa, watched him. She remembered Daagoo as a small, robust boy who always had a look of wonder on his curious face. It had been a joy to watch him eagerly explore the world around him. Now he seemed sad and preoccupied with his thoughts.

Shreenyaa remembered how she had wept when she miscarried the son before Daagoo. She and her husband had been confident that their youth and strength would protect them from harm. They were stunned by the loss of the child. Afterward, she and Ch'izhin Choo had become cautious and more reverent of life.

When Daagoo was born, they had feared they would lose him also, so they had become overprotective and indulged his wishes, instead of disciplining him. In that way they had spoiled him. Now he suffered the consequences, not understanding why they had turned against him when he needed them most. "One day," Shreenyaa told herself, "he will understand."

She called to him. "Dlak Zhuu came by earlier. She made a batch of cranberry sauce. Try some."

Daagoo grunted. He knew what his mother and Little Squirrel were doing, and he would have none of their matchmaking. Most of Daagoo's peers had been matched to girls, but he wanted to escape the responsibility already being forced on him. Marriage would end any possibility of his leaving this band to go out into the world on his own.

So he finished the food he was eating and said, "Not now. I have to rest before the hunt."

As he walked away, he heard his mother sigh. Daagoo regretted that he would never satisfy his family. His father wanted him to be a hunter, and his mother wanted grandchildren. Everything they wanted depended on him, and this burden made him miserable.

Entering his shelter, he stretched out on the bedding and stared out the doorway at the sky, watching the sun slowly go down. In summer it shined brilliantly from high in the sky, but as winter approached the sun slowly abandoned this country, leaving it cold and dark.

Looking ahead, Daagoo saw only bleakness coming with the falling snow. He imagined another intense winter struggling to survive with his people. In such times, they kept to themselves, becoming sullen and fearful. Aware that they were fighting for their lives against nature at its worst, everyone did what they were told without question. There was no time for dreams, or exploring, or even light conversation.

"How can I keep from going crazy?" he asked himself.

Daagoo did not want to cause trouble, but the more he thought about spending another winter in this land, the more depressed he became. He decided that tomorrow, after the caribou hunt, he would tell his father that he was going out on his own.

The decision would sadden his parents, but he knew that if he went along with their wishes any longer, he would become deeply enmeshed in the life of the band. He would have to abandon his dreams of following the trail of his ancestors to find out whether the legends of the Land of the Sun were true.

Daagoo took out his mooseskin map, which he always carried with him. His finger traced the path to the Land of the Sun. In his imagination he saw a country that stood green and lush, where night never turned cold, dark, and empty. The happy people of this land never heard the lonely sound of the hungry wolf crying in the night. Life was easier there, and men did not need to trudge through deep snow in search of moose that could not be found. Such a place had to exist, because the elders told such vivid stories about it. Daagoo resolved once more to find that place, and then he closed his eyes to sleep.

## CHAPTER 5
### A stubborn daughter

L eaving her parents, Bird Girl went to her shelter but did not go inside. Instead she leaned against a nearby spruce tree and calmed her thoughts. She had tried to be a good daughter. Her memories were filled with laughing male voices and her father's serious instructions. Many times she had sat looking adoringly up at him, proud to sit alone with him as he shared his knowledge of the land and animals, explaining to her how best to live life by providing for the family.

For a moment Bird Girl thought of her mother. Her heart softened at the memory of Na' Zhuu's gentle, understanding smile and the warm, wonderful meals she prepared. But Bird Girl could not begin to grasp her mother's thinking or her way of life.

Then the men of the band intruded into her thoughts. Bird Girl stood up, pacing rebelliously. She would not marry. Not now. There was so much to do. This year she had received a slight nod from her father when she begged him to let her go on the caribou hunt. She had never seen the great caribou herds. When the men hunted in the fall, Bird Girl had remained in the camp with the other women and children, but her brothers had told her about multitudes of caribou racing across the hills with the men in full pursuit. If a man had strong arms, he could bring down many caribou.

She would never get to make her first caribou kill if she married. Instead, she would have to stay with the women again, while her husband went out to hunt.

Bird Girl thought about the available men in the camp, imagining herself married to one of the boys who had always scorned her. Sometimes, if a girl was fortunate, she would be matched to one of the men in a visiting Gwich'in band. Most of the time, however, a girl was married to someone in her own band, not a close relative but someone she had known all of her life. A very unlucky girl might be matched to a man whose first wife had died, leaving him with many children. Then the new wife would be required to take care of those children as well as her own. The life of a woman was not easy.

Bird Girl envisioned herself as a married woman, caring for infant after infant, feeding them, sewing for them, cooking for them, year after year, until eventually they grew up. By then she would be an old woman whom the young people would only tolerate from a distance, for no one would have any use for her.

She had often thought that she would rather be dead than live such a life. For a moment she considered killing herself. But Bird Girl was not ready to die. She stood in the night, looking up at the star-filled sky, pondering her dilemma.

If she persuaded her parents to support her decision not to marry, her family would be ostracized. To disobey the band's decision was criminal. That was how the Gwich'in kept the peace.

A sudden hope filled her. It was possible that her family could survive on its own. She and the men were good hunters, and her mother and her brother's wives could do the other work. Bird Girl wanted to run to her father and ask him to break away from the band, but then she pictured Zhoh's stern face and knew this was only wishful thinking. Although her father and brothers had allowed her to hunt, they were traditional men and expected her to obey their people's rules.

She went into her shelter and started a fire from the embers. Waiting for the flames to reach the dry sticks on top, Bird Girl sat back and tried to think. She could refuse to marry, but then they would force her. After that there would be no turning back. Once married, most girls quickly became pregnant. Bird Girl had seen many young women moving slowly about with round bodies within a year of being matched to a man. She clearly remembered painful cries coming from outside the camp, where women went to have their babies. Sometimes, when the birth was difficult, only the midwife would return, carrying a helpless infant.

At other times an unfortunate woman would give birth to a girl and the father would order the child to be killed, for he had desired a son. Bird Girl also had witnessed the grief women suffered when a child was stillborn. She did not think she could bear life only to see it die.

More and more, Bird Girl knew she was not ready to be a wife. In a few hours the band would begin to stir, and then there would be no more waiting. Her new life would begin.

Quickly Bird Girl gathered her possessions. She did not own much aside from her bedding, her skin and fur clothing, and her weapons: bow and arrow, knife and hatchet. This was all she needed to survive.

She crept cautiously out of her shelter. If anyone saw her leaving the camp, they would raise the alarm, and she wanted to go without interruption. Perhaps, when it was understood that she was on her own and no longer obligated to her people, she would return to visit her family, or they would visit her. That was her hope.

Bird Girl moved silently across the ground among tall spruce trees that waved softly in the brisk autumn breeze. She could see the sky in the dark ripples of the ever-flowing river. When she realized she might not share the joys of the summer fishing season with her family again for a long time, her heart ached. Her love for her family was strong, but her passion to be free was stronger. She buried all thoughts of her loved ones in the back of her mind as she forced her legs to walk calmly, not run, from those who wanted to take away her freedom.

## CHAPTER 6
## The hunters

*I*n the early morning Daagoo and all the able-bodied men set out, traveling light with bows and arrows strapped to their shoulders, knives and hatchets belted to their waists, and shoulder bags filled with dried meat and fish. Their moccasined feet stepped softly on the familiar trail to the caribou grounds, high in the mountains.

Throughout the long journey, the men took turns carrying their two long canoes on their shoulders. Halfway to their destination, Daagoo

took his turn carrying one of the canoes. The craft was built of sturdy strips of spruce wood curved upward at both ends and expertly waterproofed with birch bark. After the hunt, the men would use the canoes to transport the caribou meat down a shallow, swift tributary river, back to the camp.

The hunters walked all day, then ate a meager meal and lay down to rest. At first hint of dawn's light they prepared for the hunt, setting out for the valley where the caribou grazed, a short distance farther.

Coming over a rise and down into the valley, Daagoo felt his breath taken away by the sight of hundreds of caribou spread out, pulling lichen from the ground. The men crept on all fours toward the unsuspecting animals, approaching into the wind so their scent would not be carried to the herd. All the hunters watched their leader, who signaled with his hands whether he wanted them to stop or to strike. Daagoo watched the chief and his father ahead of him, but he also watched the caribou delicately picking at the white moss. Suddenly he felt a stick under his palm, and he could not stop himself from crushing it. The twig snapped loudly.

Daagoo felt as if his heart would stop when the caribou lifted their heads. The men froze in position. After a while, the caribou relaxed. The chief turned and motioned for Daagoo to stay where he was, and the young hunter felt humiliation wash over him. His carelessness had almost cost them this hunt.

Daagoo watched as the men stealthily approached the herd. The majestic caribou looked around innocently. It saddened him that these animals must die so that his people would live.

"I will never enjoy being a hunter," Daagoo thought to himself, and for a moment, as he watched his father and the other men draw closer to the large herd, he felt regret.

Suddenly the men stood up. They thrust their spears toward their targets, then rushed forward with their knives to end the lives of the animals that had fallen in the haze of dust kicked up by the stampeding survivors.

When the chief was satisfied that they had taken enough caribou to feed the band until the next hunt, months away, Daagoo was motioned out of hiding and joined the work. The men skinned the animals, then cut up the meat. When it lay in portions, they wrapped it in caribou skins, fastening it tightly with braided rawhide rope. Then, using straps, they pulled the laden skins across the hunting grounds toward the river.

By the time this was done, it was too dark to travel by water, so they camped. Daagoo was tired, having worked hard to pay for his carelessness. He had skinned and butchered two caribou and hauled them back to the river by himself, but rather than being disheartened, he felt exhilarated. The work had given him a burst of energy, and while the other men fell asleep he lay on the ground staring restlessly up at the sky. Finally he could stand it no more.

Rising, he tiptoed out of the camp toward the river. There Daagoo found a large boulder on which he gingerly positioned himself, wrapping his arms around his legs and gazing hypnotically into the dark, velvety river, watching the stars' reflections twinkle

within the ripples and waves.

Tomorrow, after some of the men left in the canoes, he would tell his father that he could not stay and hunt with them this winter. He hoped that on the long walk back to the main camp he and his father would reconcile any harsh feelings between them.

"After all, I am a man," he said softly to himself, trying to deny the guilt he felt. "I can go out on my own anytime. I was just pleasing my parents, and they must not feel that I will stay with them forever."

Feeling sleepy, he had started back to camp when a scream filled the silence of the night. Daagoo froze, feeling the hairs on the back of his neck prickle.

Running silently toward the sound, he hid behind a grove of willows, trembling with fear, and forced himself to peek through the trees. He saw men moving around a huge fire. One of them turned, and as the flames illuminated his face, Daagoo saw that the man was an Eskimo, one of the Ch'eekwaii.

He, like the other strangers, was a large man, dressed in a light-colored jacket and knee-high moccasins. His hair was cut shoulder-length, and his face was ornamented by a bone that jutted out of the sides of his lower lip.

Chills of fear shivered through Daagoo's spine.

He watched the five Ch'eekwaii move around the camp, looking down at the Gwich'in men who lay motionless on the ground. Waves of shock ran through Daagoo as he realized that his people had been murdered in their sleep. The Ch'eekwaii must have snuck up on the sleeping men, slitting their throats before they could fight back. Daagoo stifled a sob. If the Ch'eekwaii discovered him, they would kill him, too.

Dazed, Daagoo watched as the Ch'eekwaii took their time exploring the camp, digging through the Gwich'ins' belongings. They talked excitedly when they discovered the canoes filled with caribou meat and skins. Lighting another fire away from the dead men, they cooked the meat and feasted on it. After a while, they lay down on the ground to sleep.

Only when Daagoo felt sure the last man had fallen asleep did he dare move. His legs were stiff as he slowly made his way out of hiding. Creeping through the camp, he could not help but look down at his slain people. All he saw were dark figures on the ground. A feeling of loss and emptiness overcame him. In one night his whole world had changed.

Struggling to keep from crying out in grief for the dead, he remembered the living who slept, unsuspecting, not far down the river. The Ch'eekwaii seemed in no hurry to leave this area, and they soon might discover the helpless Gwich'in women and children. He must warn them.

Daagoo thought about taking one of the canoes, but they were too close to the sleeping Ch'eekwaii. Although he knew that traveling on the river would be much faster, he could not risk being discovered.

Silently he moved away from the fire and into the darkness. By the light of the stars above, Daagoo found the trail to his people's camp and started out at a trot. All that night he ran. He did not allow himself to think, for that would fill his mind with the image of his father lying dead on the ground, unable to protect his wife and son anymore.

Soon the dawn came. Realizing how quickly the Ch'eekwaii could reach the camp, Daagoo ran in desperation. At last he smelled the smoke of campfires lingering in the early-morning air.

As Daagoo neared the camp, exhausted, an elderly woman warming herself by the campfire looked up to see him running toward her, waving his arms. "The Ch'eekwaii are coming!" he cried breathlessly. "We must flee!"

In minutes everyone in the camp was awake,

scrambling to pack their possessions. The elders gathered around Daagoo, as did young women who carried sleeping infants on their backs. Children were given large, hastily assembled bundles to carry. Daagoo had no time to pack his own belongings. Immediately he led the small group inland, away from the river. No one looked back for fear of what they might see.

## CHAPTER 7
## The hunted

F leeing her band's camp, Bird Girl walked all that day and into the night. She had no clear idea where she was going except that she was heading toward the mountains where the caribou grazed. In her mind a plan began to form. She would wait there until her people arrived for the hunt. Perhaps if she took a few caribou, they would be impressed and begin to see things her way.

Part of Bird Girl knew this was not a realistic plan, for the minds of the Gwich'in, especially the men, would never be changed. Once they decided how something should be, then that was the way it would be. Even when they allowed her to hunt, her parents had insisted that she not hunt during her menses, for fear it would bring bad times to all of their people. The relationship between animals and the spirit world was a complicated one, they had explained. Many times, Bird Girl had secretly thought of such rules as a great nuisance. Now, again, tradition was interfering with her life. For such traditions Bird Girl felt only contempt.

She would prove to her people that she could survive on her own. She would go up to those mountains and make a winter camp. There she would hunt, dry meat, and gather edible plants and berries. As she walked alongside a small river, Bird Girl's footsteps grew bold with resolve. She would show them what she could achieve without rules or traditions.

When at last the night gave way to morning, the sun began to dry the dew that weighed down the darkening yellow leaves. A few summer birds that had not yet flown south for the winter chirped in the trees. Bird Girl's steps began to drag, but she did not stop, for she knew she was not yet far enough away from her parents. The flatlands stretched for hundreds of miles, but Bird Girl's family would be able to predict where she would go — where any sensible hunter would go, to familiar hunting grounds. The band's skillful trackers would soon be on her trail.

Not until late afternoon did Bird Girl admit to herself that she needed rest. Climbing a hill next to the small river, she found a comfortable spot under a long row of tall, skinny spruce trees. From the hill she would be able to look down and see if anyone was coming.

She sat down, leaned against a tree, and closed her eyes. She could feel the warm autumn sun on her face as she fell asleep. In a while her mind drifted with the shadowy images of her parents' faces and the sound of their voices, which made her sleeping body jerk with tension.

Night came and passed, and another day began as Bird Girl slept quietly, her head lying heavily on her chest. At dawn chickadees and camp-robbers flew nearby, staring curiously with their black, shiny eyes at this invader to their territory. Ravens cawed in the distance, and tree squirrels moved busily about, pausing momentarily to glance at this woman who lay against one of their trees.

The day grew warm and silent. The small river

gurgled over its rocky bed, flowing roughly down on its way to join the wide Yuukon River in the flatlands. Tall spruce trees rose deep green against the clear blue skies, and the sun seemed to shine in satisfaction upon all that lay on this side of the earth.

As the second day wore on, the sun began to sink slowly into the west, quickly losing its heat in spite of its blazing red beauty. The air cooled in the approaching evening, and Bird Girl finally stirred. She opened her eyes and quickly looked around. She was not aware how long she had slept, but she knew that she had slept hard and it scared her. When one was alone in the wilderness, to sleep soundly was to court danger.

Her confidence shaken, Bird Girl stumbled awkwardly in the evening light as she searched the ground for twigs to build a fire. The world suddenly seemed alien to her. She forced back her fear, refusing to allow her foolish thoughts to run rampant.

Bird Girl made a fire by rubbing two dry sticks together, piling on dry leaves and grass until the sparks ignited into a flame. Then she added more dry twigs until the fire gave off enough heat for cooking. She collected big pebbles and placed them in the fire. When they were hot, she removed them from the fire with two sticks fashioned into prongs, and put them into a small birch bark bowl filled with water. As the water boiled she made it into tea by adding green leaves with golden tips, picked from a long-stemmed plant that grew near the river.

Then she sat and warmed herself, chewing on

dried moose meat and staring into the fire that lit the darkness around her. She felt an evening chill on her back and huddled closer, as if the small flames could protect her from the surrounding cold.

Drinking the minty tea, Bird Girl distracted herself from the eeriness of the night by remembering life with her people. As a little girl, she watched her mother tan moose and caribou skins, and sew them into clothing and moccasins. But when her mother tried to teach her these skills, she rebelled, running off to follow her father and brothers. Hunting and scouting the land for animals, as the men did, was more exciting than sitting for hours, concentrating on a piece of sewing. As the years passed, Zhoh taught her that hunting also required patience and concentration, but Bird Girl still preferred the work of men over the work of women.

Remembering past moose hunts with her brothers, Bird Girl wondered if she, alone, could bring down a moose. She knew her people had invented many ingenious methods to hunt animals when they were hungry. For instance, a moose could be taken by chasing it into a corral, but building a corral required teamwork, and it took great strength to push a spear through the thick hide of a moose. Women and children were only allowed to watch as the men chased the animal into the fenced area, where other hunters waited to bring down the prey.

However, one hunter might catch a large animal, such as a wolf or bear, with a pitfall trap. A snare woven from thick moose rawhide would be hung over the animal's path, waiting to catch it by the neck. Once it was caught, the weight of the animal would break the branches supporting it, and it would fall into a hidden pit. There it would die, hung by the neck.

Still, Bird Girl thought her best option was to hunt for caribou. They were smaller animals than moose, and many of them strayed from the main herd, so she would be able to bring down a few on her own. Later in the year, when animals were harder to find, she would come down from the hills and hunt smaller game.

Just a hint of light on the horizon sent Bird Girl on her way, traveling along the shallow river that flowed down from the mountains. There she planned to make her winter camp. After walking many miles toward the distant mountains, she finally began her ascent. As she climbed, she looked below and caught her breath at the vastness of the land. For a moment it made her feel small and insignificant, and she turned away for fear that she would lose her confidence in the face of it all.

Letting her eyes wander up the mountainside, she spotted what appeared to be a cave, almost concealed by thickets of willows and twisted spruce trees. Bird Girl smiled, thinking this might be her new home. The cave would take time to reach, but it would be a good vantage point from which she could see if any animal or human was approaching. Like all arctic people, Bird Girl knew to be careful in everything she did, for danger could come at any time.

Climbing the slope, Bird Girl found that the opening was smaller than it had looked. Cautiously she crawled inside as her eyes adjusted to the dimness. She gathered dry debris from the floor, brought in willow branches, and built a fire just large enough to allow her to see the inside of the cave. It was a large cavern. The ground smelled musty, and many spiderwebs tickled her face. This cave had not been used for awhile, which meant that it was safe for now. The bears had not yet begun to hibernate but might try to reclaim their home later.

In the days that followed, Bird Girl made the cave comfortable. She mixed dry goose grass from nearby lakes with young spruce boughs and spread them on the floor to replace the cave's musty smell with a deep minty scent. In the center of her dwelling she built a fireplace of rocks. Then she spent two weeks gathering a winter's supply of wood.

For tools, Bird Girl had only her weapons and a few utensils. To store food, she would need many large birch bark baskets. Normally the bark and spruce root needed to make such containers were only available in early spring. During that season the fibers were softened by the sap that loosened the bark, making it pliable and easy to work with. Now everything was hard and unbendable, ready for the long, cold winter ahead. But Bird Girl made good use of the birch bark she managed to pry from the trees, binding it together with the sinew she carried.

In the large bowls she made, Bird Girl stored berries and various edible plants left over from the summer. She also hunted ducks, rabbits, and grouse, and caught and dried salmon that had fought their way up the cold river.

Bird Girl did not allow herself to waste time thinking about her family. Instead she focused on her work. She was there to prove that she could survive, and that was all that mattered. When the snow arrived and the bitter cold forced her to spend long hours inside her cave, she would have plenty of time to contemplate her future.

Soon Bird Girl had stocked her cave with food. She also filled the caches she had built, cage-like wooden containers hidden high in the trees where animals could not reach them.

Finally it was time for her first caribou hunt. The days were still warm despite the cold nights and frozen lakes, but looking up at the snow-covered mountaintops Bird Girl knew winter would come soon. When the leaves had fallen, she set out for the mountains that the men from her band had described as the place where they hunted for caribou.

Recalling how excitedly the men had talked and laughed about the caribou hunt, Bird Girl had misgivings for a few moments. The band had always been so happy after such a hunt, everyone seeming to think as one as they feasted on the caribou meat. Then Bird Girl caught herself and, with some effort, pushed those wistful thoughts from her mind.

As she walked on, it occurred to her that she had almost become a naa'in. Bird Girl remembered the elders' stories about men who wandered the wilderness. Now she understood who these men might be:

people like herself, people who did not fit into a band and had to leave. Often they were shunned for dis-obedience or refusing to work. After these men left their band, no other bands would welcome them. Such people only disturbed the harmony of a band, and lack of harmony was a threat to survival.

So naa'ins resorted to sneaking in and out of camps, stealing food, sometimes stealing women or children, or just spying on people from behind bushes, trying to rid themselves of their terrible loneliness. Eventually the naa'ins came to be considered non-living beings, more spirit than human. Anyone who saw one would speak of his ghost-like behavior.

Bird Girl did not want to become a naa'in. She would try to keep in touch with her family. But for now they must be allowed to think about her disappearance. When they realized what a good hunter she had been, perhaps they would allow her to return on her conditions.

The walk was long, and the day pleasant and clear. Bird Girl paced herself, resting for the night near the rushing river. The next day she rose early. As she continued her ascent into the steep mountains, she could see her breath in the cold air and hear the crunch of frost beneath her feet. When she reached

the top of one slope, she paused to survey the hills below and the craggy mountaintops ahead. Soon these mountains would be impassable with snow.

She walked along a plateau, hoping that the caribou would be grazing somewhere nearby. She had heard stories that the caribou were so plentiful that even an unskilled hunter could bring down at least two before the herd took off in a stampede. Her heart raced. She felt sure that, when the time came, she would bring down more than that.

Suddenly, following a ridge down into a valley, she saw hundreds of caribou below. In awe she watched the animals graze amidst a quiet hum of activity. Bird Girl had not been prepared for this sight. Gone was all her determination to hunt these animals. She sat on the ground, absorbed in the magnificent view.

Then her eye caught a movement above the grazing caribou. She focused on it and saw men sneaking up on the herd. They moved stealthily, hidden beneath caribou skins that blended into the tan grass and the dry brown ground.

Eventually the caribou picked up the scent of their human predators and became restless. Before they could take flight, the men under the skins stood up, throwing their spears. The caribou stampeded in a thunderous race for their lives.

Bird Girl stared in admiration at the many caribou the hunters brought down. Who were these hunters? Were they her people? Excited to see them nearby, she realized how much she missed her people, especially her family. Was she ready to accept their rules after all?

As Bird Girl sat there thinking, she realized she had been spotted by one of the men below. He began to trot toward her.

The hair on the nape of her neck began to prickle in alarm. Something was not right. She could not be sure from this distance, but Bird Girl sensed that these were not her people.

Instead of running away she continued to stare as if in a trance, trying to pinpoint what was different about the approaching figure. Perhaps it was the way he ran. He moved not as a friend coming in greeting but as a predator moving in on its prey. But only when Bird Girl saw the man's foreign clothing — he wore not the tan mooseskin shirt of the Gwich'in, but a white skin jacket — did she realize that he might be one of her people's enemies from far across the mountains.

Her heart beat rapidly as she remembered the many stories she had heard about the Ch'eekwaii and Gwich'in fighting over hunting grounds. The Ch'eekwaii, Bird Girl had been told, killed many innocent people. As a young girl she had been frightened of an elderly man in her band because of his scarred appearance. The Ch'eekwaii had captured him and mutilated his face to show the Gwich'in what happened to those who trespassed into their territory.

Growing up, Bird Girl stopped paying attention to these stories. Now, as she sat transfixed, the legends came back to her. When she clearly saw that the man was a foreigner, she jumped up and fled in panic.

In all the years she had been trained to run and leap over fallen trees, her legs had never failed her, but they did now. It was as if the ground became her worst enemy as she stumbled and fell many times. Fright paralyzed her mind and her body.

Without looking, Bird Girl knew with a fearsome certainty that the man was gaining on her. She gasped for air, running with all her strength, but heard the man's footsteps hitting the ground hard as he drew closer. Before she could stop herself, she turned to look and stumbled again. The man closed in quickly.

Bird Girl froze in horror at his appearance. He was tall, and the closer he came, the taller he seemed. His stern face was decorated by a narrow bone ornament jutting out of the sides of his lower lip. Bird Girl felt sure that he could not be human.

She rose and turned to run again, but the Ch'eekwaii leaped forward with such force that he caught her roughly and fell hard on top of her, knocking the breath from her body. Darkness clouded Bird Girl's senses as she fought for air. She struggled, but the man held her roughly with one hand. A cruel look came over his face as he stared at her.

The Ch'eekwaii's memories were long, and the tall hunter could still envision the day when, as a boy, he had first encountered these people. He and his father had been hunting caribou on the foothills of the tundra when they spotted the intruders. Suspecting they might kill him, the father hid his son behind a shrub and told him not to move. From there the boy had watched as the Gwich'in raiders clubbed his father to death.

Never would he forget that day. As a child he had been taught to hate his tribal enemies through the many stories he had heard about their cruelty. The murder of his father made that hatred real.

Now he held one of the Gwich'in in his hands. This girl continued to struggle even though she knew she was beaten, and he felt contempt for her audacity. How dare she think she could beat him! He easily twisted her arm until she winced.

Bird Girl saw the man's malicious smile. She leaned over and bit into his hand until she tasted her enemy's blood. The man yowled in pain, but before Bird Girl could savor her small victory he hit her hard with his fist, and she knew only blackness.

## CHAPTER 8
### A race for survival

*A*ll that day Daagoo led his band down the path away from their camp. When the people complained about not being allowed to rest, he reminded them that the Ch'eekwaii men might be following them. As they stumbled after him, the women questioned Daagoo about the missing men. He refused to answer, not wanting to speak or think about what had happened. He would tell them later, when they were safe — not now.

Night came, and the band moved quietly

through the darkness, except for a few children who whimpered. Finally Daagoo recognized a secluded area that he knew was close to the Yuukon. They still had miles to go, but they needed rest.

"We will camp here for the night," he said.

Everyone except Daagoo dropped exhausted to the ground and slept. He would not allow himself to sleep. The memory of the dead men on the ground was too fresh in his mind. He wondered where the Ch'eekwaii were and whether they had found the camp. Did they suspect that the band had escaped? Were they close behind? If the Ch'eekwaii caught up with his people, they would have to fight, but this group of women, children, and old men was no match for five strong Ch'eekwaii.

When the people awoke, Daagoo allowed them to eat a small meal of dried moose meat with fat. As soon as they finished, he told them they had to leave right away. They protested, wanting an explanation, but Daagoo only reminded them that the Ch'eekwaii could easily overtake them, covering much of the distance quickly by riding downriver in the canoes. The band did not argue with Daagoo, for he no longer seemed to be a carefree boy. Overnight he had become a man, desperate and demanding.

That day Daagoo led his people toward the Yuukon River, where they paused long enough to eat and rest. At dusk on the second day, Daagoo decided that they had traveled far enough that the Ch'eekwaii would not find them. He allowed the band to camp, and he sat down to rest. Unable to stop himself, he fell asleep.

Daagoo slept through the night and well into the next day. When he awoke, the autumn sun was high in the sky. Daagoo basked in the clear air just beginning to warm. He heard someone moving about. Opening his eyes, he was startled to see many people sitting in a circle around him.

"What is it?" he asked, embarrassed that they had been watching him sleep.

His mother spoke first.

"You will tell us what happened," Shreenyaa said firmly, her voice low.

Daagoo knew he could no longer hold back the truth. The women whose husbands and sons were missing sat close to him, pleading with their eyes for him to deny their worst fears. He realized that they already knew what had happened, but they needed to hear him say it before they could believe it was true.

He took a deep breath. "All of them were killed by the Ch'eekwaii."

The women began to grieve, some stifling their sobs with their hands and rushing away to cry, others sitting and weeping openly. Daagoo looked to his mother for reassurance and saw tears sliding down her cheeks.

He felt his own tears fall. Never had he seen such despair. The events of the past few days overwhelmed him, and he did not know how to respond to this sorrow. Instead, he closed his eyes and turned his back to them.

After a moment, he looked up at the blue sky. Behind him was greater pain than he had ever known. He was not prepared for this, but his people needed him. He was the only able-bodied hunter left. The four other adult men in the band were very old. There were some young boys, but they did not possess the size or the strength to run fast, or to kill a large animal and haul it a long distance.

The responsibility of being the band's leader lay upon Daagoo, and he felt the weight of it already. "How can I be their leader when I can barely contain my own pain?" he asked himself.

Then a hand touched his shoulder. He turned to look into the eyes of his mother. "Son, do not be afraid," Shreenyaa said.

Daagoo looked shamefully around to see if the others had heard. He was too proud to admit that he felt helpless.

"I am not, Mother," he said in a strained voice, but she smiled knowingly and patted his shoulder.

Taking a deep breath, Daagoo turned back toward the band. He and the four elderly men gathered into a pile all the bags of supplies that the people had brought with them from their old camp. Then the old men looked at Daagoo, waiting. He realized that from then on they would always wait for him to make the first move. That was what it meant to be a leader, he supposed.

He knelt down and opened the bags one by one. Inside were six hatchets, ten knives, a few bundles of dried moose meat and dried salmon, some skeins of sinew, six large pieces of raw moose hide, four fur blankets, needles and sewing awls, one pair of moccasins, and a flint.

Daagoo shook his head in disbelief. By this time of year, his band had usually stockpiled great quantities of dried fish and smoked caribou and moose meat to sustain them through the long, deadly winter. Now, not long before the first snowfall, they were almost without supplies. It was too risky to return to their campsite to retrieve more belongings. Besides, the Ch'eekwaii had probably been there already, taking what they could and burning the rest.

One of the elderly men sensed Daagoo's uncertainty.

"Do not be afraid," he said in a low voice. "We will help you along the way. You are not alone."

Daagoo did not respond. When it came to dealing with people he felt lost, for he had always been a loner. He understood more about the land and animals than about people. Now the women and their families watched him in expectation. Daagoo could not help but resent their sudden dependence on him.

"This is to be my plight from now on," he said to himself. "I am not to have time to grieve for my own loss. I must do this task set before me and save my own feelings for later."

Daagoo's first job was to explain to the young boys that they would have to become hunters, and possibly warriors, like their fathers and brothers who had died. The boys looked up at him earnestly, frightened but determined to do their best.

"It will not be long before winter comes," Daagoo told them. "We will have to work hard to replace the things we left behind. There will be little time to train you in the ways of the animals, but I hope you listened carefully to your fathers and will use what they taught you."

As Daagoo spoke, he saw his father's face. How many times had his father spoken to him sharply, trying to call him out of his daydreaming? Often when Ch'izhin Choo had tried to teach him something, Daagoo had only nodded his head, pretending to listen. Now Daagoo wondered how much he and the others would suffer for that.

The following days were busy ones in the new camp. The older women tore dry bark from the birch trees and, weaving it together with strips of sinew, made many bowls for cooking and storing food. Younger women scavenged the area in search of berries, edible plants, and rose hips left over from the summer. Even the youngest children were put to work, collecting loose wood and tree fungus, which burned slowly and would keep their fires lit throughout the winter.

Meanwhile, the four elderly men cut down young spruce trees and split the wood into thin slices, which they bent into frames for snowshoes. They soaked rawhide moose skin in water to soften it, then cut it into strips and wove it into the snowshoes. The old men also used the spruce wood to make long spears, bows, and arrows.

As these weapons were finished, Daagoo used them to train the boys to shoot. Most of the boys learned easily, for they had watched their fathers and older brothers, and many had begun to practice already. But they lacked the strength to shoot heavy arrows with any real impact. Daagoo knew that if any large animals were to be caught, he would have to do the killing.

When he felt they were ready, Daagoo decided to take the young boys on a hunt for moose. The women had used snares to catch rabbits and squirrels, and they fed the small band of hunters well to strengthen them for the journey.

As the hunting party set out, Daagoo recognized the mountains ahead of them as the ones he had longed to explore. He led the group toward these mountains, but they saw no animals except tree squirrels and a variety of birds.

All that day they walked, and still no game was to be found. Turning around, Daagoo saw that he was far ahead of the boys. With impatience he beckoned them to hurry. They had been taught not to complain and followed his instructions as best they could. Finally, well into the night, Daagoo called them to a halt. The boys gratefully lay down to rest.

Daagoo stood guard while the young hunters slept. He looked up at the glistening stars, and the vastness of the night sky made him feel insignificant. Struggling to rid himself of the feeling, Daagoo turned his thoughts to his mother. He worried about her and the other women he had left behind. What if the Ch'eekwaii had followed them to the Yuukon? What if he and the boys returned to find all the women and children slain?

For a moment Daagoo almost roused the boys, intending to go back, but instead he forced himself to relax. These were just foolish worries. The Ch'eekwaii would not still be in this territory with winter coming on.

His mind drifted back to the night when he had lost his father. "I must not cry," he told himself. "Not now. Perhaps later." But Daagoo recalled every detail of the day when he and his father had knelt side by side cutting caribou meat, and of the night when he had sat by the river, wondering how to tell his father he was leaving. He could almost see the shadows slinking within that dark night, and hear the sharp, death-filled cry that he would never forget.

If it had not been for that cry, Daagoo would have walked into his death. "I owe that man my life," he thought. And because he did not know which man had cried out to warn him, Daagoo was indebted to them all. In return he must care for all their families. Before he fell asleep that night, Daagoo resolved to put aside his own desires and do his best to help the band survive, as his father had taught him.

In spite of his vow to be more responsible, Daagoo slept late into the morning. The boys hesitated before they dared to wake him. Daagoo looked up at the sun and saw it was well into the sky.

"Why did you not wake me earlier?" he demanded, scowling. Without giving them time to answer, he rushed the young boys on to the day's hunt. "Remember, animals move around when they are hungry. In the early morning they search for food and water. We may have missed our chance, but we will look anyway." The boys nodded as they silently followed.

It was an unusually warm day, and as the hunters walked they paused many times to drink from the streams they followed. In the late afternoon, just as they were about to round a bend in a creek, they saw a large moose.

Daagoo motioned the boys to be still, then moved quietly along the side of the creek hidden by over-hanging willows. When he thought he was close enough, he fitted an arrow into his bow, pulled it back tight, took aim, and let go.

A whish sound filled the air as the arrow flew to its target, hitting hard in the animal's side. The moose was surprised. Its body buckled slightly, but when it saw Daagoo coming toward it, loading another arrow, the moose turned and ran.

In large strides it picked up speed. Not wanting the wounded animal to escape, Daagoo quickened his pace, shot, and caught the moose's right hind leg. Again the animal swayed but, determined to get away, it regained its balance and ran shakily. Daagoo shot more arrows futilely. Then, drawing closer, he shot his last arrow, and it penetrated the moose's vital innards.

The animal toppled. Before it could rise, Daagoo was on top of it, his sharp knife cutting deep into the moose's flesh, severing the thick veins in its neck. The moose twitched vio-lently as its life ebbed away, and Daagoo was thrown to the ground. He jumped up, ready to defend himself if the moose rose once more, but the animal lay still.

The boys ran up to Daagoo, impressed with what their leader had done. Daagoo was overwhelmed with excitement but managed to hide it, taking control of his emotions to instruct the boys on how to butcher the moose.

First they took out the guts and cut the neck from the body. Then Daagoo skinned the animal. Next he told the boys to take off the front legs and the back legs. Unaccustomed to this kind of work but determined, the young hunters obeyed, removing the legs and cutting apart first the front of the body, then the back.

Daagoo pondered how to transport all the moose meat back to their camp. He decided to dry the meat, which would make it lighter to carry. The hunters built a hut-like wooden frame, which they covered with willow branches. There they hung the quartered meat, building a fire underneath it, and allowing the meat to dry in the smoke.

After a few days, when the blood in the meat had dried, Daagoo ordered two boys to return to the camp and bring back five of the strongest women. Worried that the boys might get lost, he drew a map in the dirt, showing them what landmarks to look for and which creeks to follow.

"This is all part of your training," he told them, and the children nodded solemnly.

The next night the women arrived. Each had brought a rope of babiche, thickly stripped raw moose hide, with which to tie the meat onto her back. Daagoo gave small yet heavy pieces of meat to the boys to carry on their backs, and gave larger portions to the women. The rest of the meat he hung in caches high in the trees, where wolves and other predators could not reach it. Small camp-robbers and ravens would pick at the meat but would not do much damage.

The walk back was long and difficult, but neither the women nor the boys complained. They understood that the meat they carried would mean their survival. When they arrived at the camp, it was late at night but some of those left behind had remained awake in case the hunters returned. After the women and boys put down their loads of moose meat, they were fed whitefish meat and broth.

Daagoo and the boys rested, for they would have to haul more meat the following day. It took a few more trips to transport it all, but as the meat arrived, a cheerful mood spread through the camp. However, Daagoo still worried. He knew the band's chances of surviving the winter were slim.

Daagoo thought back to the caribou hunt when the Ch'eekwaii had attacked. Usually when the band hunted, a few of the strong men were left behind to protect the women and children, but that time all the men had gone on the hunt because they wanted to bring back as much meat as possible. No one had considered that the Ch'eekwaii might trespass into their territory.

Daagoo tried to comprehend why this had happened. Why had the Ch'eekwaii killed his father and the other men? What did they want? He knew that the two peoples had come to hate each other, but he had not understood the destructive power of such hatred. Whatever the reason for the raid, Daagoo knew that he would never again take his people's safety for granted.

Soon Daagoo and his hunters brought down another moose. The meat from this bull was lean from the time it had spent in the rutting season, but they had to content themselves with whatever meat they caught, for winter was fast approaching.

The small band built their winter camp near the

mighty Yuukon. Small huts of wood and moss were constructed along its banks, and the people knew not an idle moment as they foraged for wood and food. Daagoo spent each day scouting for large game, but he and his young hunters found only the small animals that the women were catching: ptarmigan, rabbits, squirrels, ducks, muskrats, and beaver. The women also set a trap in a nearby stream and caught many whitefish, which they dried.

Besides food, the band needed more warm clothing. Every piece of fur or skin the women found was turned into clothes or blankets. The skins from the two moose were tanned and fashioned into mittens and the bottoms of fur boots. While the women tanned and sewed, Daagoo and the elders made more tools, building knives and hatchets of spruce wood and moose bones.

Frost settled in, then the snow fell. Daagoo and his people finally were secure in their shelters. The following months were not as hard as Daagoo had envisioned. The band subsisted on their stores of food, also snaring rabbits in the snow and spearing fish through holes in the river ice.

Daagoo kept himself busy and tried not to think of his lost dream to follow the sun. Instead, as the winter wore on, he became more hopeful about the band's future. Soon the young boys would be men and the girls would become women. In time, more Gwich'in would be born and the band would grow again. However, this did not much cheer Daagoo, who realized that he was more trapped in this way of life than ever before.

## CHAPTER 9
## Captured

B ird Girl awoke with her head upside down. In a fog of pain, she realized she was being carried over the shoulder of her captor as if she were a large piece of caribou meat wrapped in its own hide. Her hands and feet were tightly bound; a strip of skin had been tied over her mouth. She felt suffocated and trapped. For a brief moment, she knew what an animal must feel when it is about to die.

The Ch'eekwaii hunters walked a long distance

that day. When they stopped, the man dropped Bird Girl carelessly. Although her body hit the ground hard, she allowed no pain to show on her face. Instead she kept her eyes closed so the men would not know she was awake.

The hunters rested briefly, and then Bird Girl felt herself being lifted abruptly off the ground by her captor. The other men carried meat-laden packs on their backs, and pulled behind them hunks of meat rolled inside caribou skins, the fur side down to help it slide across the hard ground. Their loads were heavy, but these men, bred in a harsh land devoid of trees where life was etched out of ice and snow, thought nothing of such hard work.

One day passed, then another, as Bird Girl was carried through the mountains. The hunter who had captured her, called Turak by the other Ch'eekwaii, gave her no opportunity to escape. When he needed to rest and put her down, he kept a close eye on her even though she was tightly bound with strips of tanned hide. Bird Girl quickly learned not to look Turak in the eye. Once, when he caught her staring at him, he picked up a bone from the meat he had been eating and threw it at her face.

The men slept fitfully each night and each morning

YUUKON

Gwichyaa Zheh

J. L. Grant

resumed their journey north, through the mountain passes, toward their homeland. As they walked, the other Ch'eekwaii occasionally glanced at the Gwich'in woman that their leader carried.

Turak had led them into Gwich'in territory, and as he ventured farther inland, they had not objected. They respected him as a capable hunter and feared him as a warrior, knowing how brutal he could become when anyone crossed him. Although they had hoped to avoid an encounter with their enemies, Turak seemed to hunger for such a confrontation. The other Ch'eekwaii knew what deep hatred Turak had for the Gwich'in, having heard the story about his father's murder. Now, although she was one of their enemies, the hunters could not help but feel some sympathy for the Gwich'in woman. As Turak's possession, she would be shown no mercy.

When they were out of Gwich'in territory, Turak dropped Bird Girl roughly to the ground and cut the bonds around her feet. Then he pulled her up and forced her to walk on her numb, weakened legs. Trudging through the mountains, Bird Girl became more and more disheartened. Her family would never suspect that she had been kidnapped. How could she hope for rescue?

Days passed, and still Turak did not feed her. Occasionally one of the other hunters risked their leader's anger by giving her a drink of water when Turak was not around. When her belly growled for food, and her mouth became dry and parched, Bird Girl began to stumble in her weakness. Then Turak became angry and impatient, slapping her on the side of the head until she could not think clearly.

Finally, the small group of Ch'eekwaii hunters came down from the mountains with their caribou meat and their captive. Through a daze of misery, Bird Girl looked down and saw a land that lay flat, brown, and empty from one horizon to the other. Wind blew the smell of tundra moss into her nostrils.

The men became more lively and talkative as they reached the open country, but inwardly Bird Girl shrank back from this barren land. She wanted to throw herself on the ground and refuse to move any farther. Instead she continued to walk mindlessly. She had no strength left to fight.

After crossing many miles of foothills and tundra, the travelers neared an encampment that stood out against the low horizon. Domed shelters rose out of the ground, covered in sod. Throughout the camp were scattered sleds and overturned fishing boats.

Dogs with thick ruffs stood tied to the shelters, bark-
ing. Clothing, hung on poles between the shelters,
flapped noisily in the breeze. Beyond the camp lay an
endless expanse of water, and Bird Girl felt its salty
moisture in the air, stinging her eyes.

Seeing people in the camp, she took a deep breath, willing herself to be brave. The Ch'eekwaii greeted their hunters with great excitement, but there came a long silence when they saw the captive. They had heard stories about their enemies to the south, although most had never seen them. This girl did not look like the terrible foe they had been taught to fear.

The hunters disappeared into their shelters, leaving Bird Girl standing in the middle of a gathering crowd. She dared not look directly at the Ch'eekwaii people, but caught glimpses of their strange-looking faces, some tattooed with lines and circles, others decorated with bone ornaments. They wore white skin tunics and pants, some carrying knives. Bird Girl was terrified, not knowing what they would do to her.

They continued to stare at her, gradually coming closer. A few amused themselves by poking at her. One man sniffed at her loudly, causing great laughter when he made a face of disgust. Bird Girl felt her cheeks burn in humiliation.

When they decided she was harmless, the Ch'eekwaii lost interest in her and one by one returned to their shelters. Bird Girl stood for a long time, not knowing what was expected of her. No one seemed to care what she did. She wondered if she should try to escape. The water lay before her and the mountains lay behind her. All she had to do was run toward those faraway mountains. On the other side was her land, her people.

Yet as she stood there, a lone Gwich'in woman, the wind whipping against her hair, Bird Girl lost her courage. Between her and the mountains lay many miles of flat land, with no trees to hide her. If she ran, the Ch'eekwaii would recapture her easily. She imagined them hunting her down and killing her, and fear kept her rooted to the ground.

She did not move, even as the light faded. The wind from the sea picked up into a gusting howl that left her damp and chilled through her skin clothing. As she stood there on the tundra, lost and confused, a small, slightly bent old woman came out of a shelter. Bird Girl braced herself as the woman came near, but the woman walked past her into the twilight, probably to relieve her bladder, Bird Girl thought.

In a short time, the elderly woman returned and stopped in surprise, for she had not been present earlier when the hunters had brought Bird Girl into the camp. Looking to see if anyone else was around, she slowly approached the Gwich'in girl.

The Ch'eekwaii woman studied Bird Girl from

head to toe, muttering in disbelief. The woman appeared to be very old, yet she moved with agility. Looking up at Bird Girl, who stood a head taller than she, the woman asked a question in a direct tone. Bird Girl held out her hands helplessly, for she understood not one word.

The woman rattled on, and Bird Girl tried to understand the words that clicked and rolled in one long monotone after another. The woman became excited and angry, pointing to the sod houses. At last she threw up her hands in exasperation. Then, much to Bird Girl's astonishment, the old woman beckoned the girl into her shelter.

It took Bird Girl a moment to respond, and the woman became impatient, yelling something in the Ch'eekwaii language. Not wanting to bring this woman's anger on herself, Bird Girl hurried to follow.

She bent her head to step through the shelter's entrance, a low tunnel with skins hanging down to serve as inner and outer doors. Inside, the walls were covered with caribou skins sewn together with the hair left on, probably for warmth, Bird Girl thought. Looking at it from the outside, she would not have imagined how spacious this dwelling was inside. It was brightly lit and evenly heated by a lamp carved of soapstone, holding a lit wick floating in whale oil. Small holes in the top of the shelter allowed the smoke from the lamp to escape.

While Bird Girl looked around, the Ch'eekwaii woman went to a caribou skin bedding at one side of the room and lay down on it, ignoring her visitor. The only place for Bird Girl to sleep was on the hard ground. It did not look appealing, but she was tired and feared she might not be given another opportunity to rest. She stretched out on the floor and looked up at the ceiling, listening to the old woman snore.

The oil lamp cast a soft, wavering glow throughout the dwelling. Bird Girl tried to sleep, but thoughts of escape filled her mind. The Ch'eekwaii, knowing she was a stranger to this country, must have assumed that she would not run away for fear of getting lost. Bird Girl knew she was wasting a chance to escape, but again her fear took control. Her body was weakened by lack of food and water, and she desperately needed sleep. If she ran now, she would probably die from cold and exhaustion. Even if she survived crossing the tundra, she would not know how to find the pass that lead through the mountains. For now, she would wait. When she was strong again and knew where to run, then she would escape.

Bird Girl slept restlessly as her stomach growled for food. In the morning, she awoke to find the elderly woman warming her hands over the oil lamp and taking bites from a piece of dried meat. Bird Girl's mouth watered at the sight, but the woman ignored her. Bird Girl wondered how to get some of the food. She had not been a prisoner long, but already she had learned that nothing would be given to her freely.

Then the woman surprised her by throwing her a piece of meat. Bird Girl took it cautiously and began to chew on it. The meat had a tart taste rich with animal oil. Bird Girl chewed slowly, trying not to make a face, for she knew that the oils were what her body needed most. The woman did not look at her directly but motioned for her to drink from a skin flask. Bird Girl obeyed, savoring the cold water.

The two women, young and old, Gwich'in and Ch'eekwaii, ate together in silence until suddenly, with a great rumble, Turak burst into the shelter. He grabbed Bird Girl roughly by the wrist, shouting and waving a clenched fist at the elderly woman, who shrugged, hardly acknowledging his presence.

In frustration, Turak turned his attention to Bird Girl, slapping her hard on the side of the head, then dragging her out of the shelter. She screamed in pain and he hit her again, pulling her across the ground and into his dwelling as if she weighed nothing.

There the big Ch'eekwaii raved at her in his harsh-sounding tongue, pointing at her angrily. When his captive could not grasp what he wanted, he became even more furious and hit her again. Bird Girl finally guessed that he wanted her to clean his shelter, and she quickly knelt down to pick up pieces of clothing that had been strewn carelessly across the floor. When he was satisfied, Turak left Bird Girl with a pounding headache and a deep sense of loss.

Soon it became clear that Bird Girl was to live with Turak and serve as his slave. As the days passed in the land of her enemies, Bird Girl saw how Turak was respected and feared by everyone in the camp, except, perhaps, the stubborn old woman. Like Bird Girl's people, the Ch'eekwaii revered the strong hunters who sustained their lives by providing food. So when they saw Turak beat his slave on the head for making the smallest mistake, they looked the other way.

In time Turak claimed Bird Girl as a wife, ripping into her brutally. He seemed pleased that he had bloodied her, smiling cruelly as she fought to choke back her sobs. Long after he fell asleep, she lay awake, anguishing over her awful mistake. She had run away from her own people to avoid marriage. Now she was in the hands of an enemy and suffering a fate that was far worse.

## CHAPTER 10
### "We have to trust in our future"

*In the midst of winter, when a few cold spells had come and gone and much snow had fallen, the sun lay low on the horizon one day when some of the children came running into Daagoo's camp, shouting that a group of men were approaching.*

*Daagoo, who had been sharpening his spear, jumped to his feet. Cold fear gripped him. Mothers rushed their children into shelters. Although the young hunters and women came forward armed with weapons, Daagoo felt helpless, knowing they* were not strong enough for a fight.

He watched grimly as the men came closer, walking along the riverbank. There were only three of them, and Daagoo guessed that his people might have a chance of overtaking them. He stood in front of the camp with the boys and women behind him. As the strangers drew closer, Daagoo could tell from their clothing that they were Gwich'in. Still, he did not relax, for in the harsh winter a relative could be as deadly as a known enemy.

"We mean you no harm. We are friends," one of the strangers called out. "We are looking for one of our people."

Daagoo wondered what to do. Since his father's death, he had little faith in other people. Still, these men looked friendly. After a moment, he answered, "Stay there. I will come to you." He walked warily toward the men.

Quickly one of them said, "We are looking for our sister. She left our camp weeks ago and has not been seen since."

Daagoo relaxed slightly because the man spoke in his dialect. These were close relatives.

"We have not seen anyone around here," he answered.

There was not much else to say, but they did not leave. Finally, out of courtesy, Daagoo invited them to rest by the campfire before they continued their journey.

As the men sat down near the fire, Daagoo wondered whether it had been a mistake to invite them into camp. He watched them with suspicion. "If your sister left weeks ago, why are you looking for her now?" he asked.

The men exchanged glances. One of them gave a long sigh. "Bird Girl is very independent," he explained. "She was being forced to marry and left our camp the night before our father was to choose a man for her. We thought she needed time to herself and would return. Now weeks have gone by, and our parents are worried. They sent us out to find her."

Another of the brothers noticed that Daagoo seemed surprised to hear the girl's name. "Have you seen her?" he asked Daagoo.

Daagoo hesitated. "I think I met your sister once, along the river. She said she was hunting, but it sounded as if she planned to return to her people."

The brothers decided that Daagoo must have met their sister sometime before she ran away. They knew Daagoo could not help them find her, but curiosity held them a moment longer. They thought it strange that, in this band of many women and children, Daagoo was the only grown man. He did not seem to have the maturity or confidence of a chief. Cautiously, one of the brothers asked, "Where are your men?"

Daagoo thought for a few moments before answering. He had no reason to trust these men. Yet he wanted to trust them, for he was tired of carrying the burden of his people's tragedy by himself. Before he could change his mind, he blurted out, "They were killed by the Ch'eekwaii, up at the caribou crossing."

"When did this happen?" the man asked.

Daagoo found himself describing everything that had happened. After he finished, Daagoo watched nervously as the brothers huddled together, speaking in low voices. Worried, Daagoo looked toward his band. His mother smiled reassuringly and shrugged her shoulders. Daagoo returned a weak smile, not sharing her confidence.

Finally the three men turned their attention back to Daagoo. "My brothers and I think that you should join our band," one said. Daagoo heard his people whispering excitedly.

The man held up his hands to quiet them. "I have

more to say. It is good you have survived this disaster. You have been brave, but you know it takes more than bravery to survive in this land. It takes a great number of people working together. This is how the Gwich'in have endured.

"Our band has a good chief. He is a fair man and has been a good leader for half his life. He and the rest of our people will welcome you."

Daagoo felt his throat tighten with emotion. His band was being offered a new future. But Daagoo forced himself to calm down. He could not make this decision alone.

"I need to discuss this with my people," he told the three brothers. They agreed and walked a short distance from the camp, giving the band its privacy.

"What do you think?" Daagoo asked, looking at his mother.

Shreenyaa also had been taken by surprise and did not know what to say. Then one of the elderly men spoke.

"I am proud of you, Daagoo, for being a good leader," he said. "I feel confident that we can survive this winter even if we do not accept this offer. But the women should find new husbands and the children need fathers, men who will teach them. We are so busy struggling to survive that our boys are missing much of their training."

Daagoo's mother nodded in agreement. "He is right," she said. "We need more people for a better chance. That is how it should be."

Many of the other adults agreed, but some were unsure. Daagoo also felt uncertain. Everything was happening so swiftly, and he was afraid of making the wrong choice.

"I do not know what to do," he told the band. "I do not want to make a decision for all of you and later regret it. You must decide for yourselves. We do not know these people. If we join them, we will have to trust them completely."

The people nodded their heads and began to talk among themselves. Meanwhile, Daagoo turned his attention to the brothers, wondering about their sister. Was she still alive? It was difficult to live in the wilderness alone. Even a wolf had less chance of survival when he was forced from the pack, so how could a young girl survive?

As Daagoo's mind began to wander, his mother called to him. She spoke for the people.

"We will join this band," Shreenyaa announced. "We have to trust in our future. We could continue to live on our own, but it would be difficult and dangerous. It is better to have more men in case we need to protect ourselves."

The three brothers' faces broke into smiles. "You will not regret your decision," one said. Daagoo's people smiled back warmly.

The next morning the eldest of Bird Girl's brothers returned to his people to tell them about Daagoo's band. Meanwhile, the two younger brothers helped Daagoo and the others prepare for the journey. The older brother reappeared two days later, bringing word that the chief and his people eagerly awaited the arrival of their new family. Packing his belongings, Daagoo felt a great relief, as if a heavy burden had been lifted from his shoulders.

The small band walked through the snow for several days to reach the new camp. There a large number of friendly Gwich'in people greeted them, making them feel at home as they set up shelters. Soon children were busy meeting other children, and women were talking to their new neighbors. As Daagoo watched, he felt a tenderness for his people. He had not seen them so happy for a long time.

One day, a few weeks later, Daagoo was following a trail, scouting for small game, when he met the three brothers. He knew they often left the camp for days, looking for Bird Girl. He offered to help them, but they said no.

"She is our sister," one said. "It is our responsibility to find her."

Daagoo was disappointed. He was eager to join the search for the girl because it would give him an excuse to explore the countryside, but out of respect for the brothers he did not argue with them.

Months later, when the winter snow was melting away, Daagoo heard that the brothers had found Bird Girl's belongings in a cave near Ch'eekwaii country. If she had been killed by an animal, her clothing or some remains would have been left, but none was found. Bird Girl's mother cried out in despair, while her father stood by with a grim face, blaming himself. The three brothers and their wives hung their heads in sorrow. No one doubted that Bird Girl had been kidnapped or killed by the Ch'eekwaii.

Daagoo longed to comfort them, but instead he stayed at a polite distance. Like the rest of the band, he could only stand by helplessly as the proud family grieved.

After they had finished weeping, the brothers vowed that they would not give up their search. They were determined to discover a way through the mountains, to find the guilty Ch'eekwaii, and to rescue or avenge their sister. Hearing this, Daagoo offered to go with them. Again they refused his help.

Restlessly, Daagoo watched them pack a few belongings and set out across the flatlands, heading for the distant mountains to the north.

## CHAPTER 11
## Life among the enemy

B ird Girl soon learned the patterns of her new life as a slave of the Ch'eekwaii. During the days when Turak hunted with the other men, the women kept her busy with work. Any resistance only invited more beatings, so she acted submissive, trying to do whatever they wanted. Sometimes she could not understand their words and gestures, and that brought an angry stick across her bottom or a slap to her face. Eventually Bird Girl learned some of the Ch'eekwaii words, enough to comprehend their demands and insults.

The Ch'eekwaii would never let her forget she was their enemy, no matter how hard she tried to appease them. The women allowed their children to tease her and to throw things at her as they watched, amused. Bird Girl bit her lip and fought back her tears, vowing they would never see her cry.

To further torment her, they often refused to give her anything to eat. Although most of their food was unpleasantly foreign, Bird Girl was always hungry for it. When she helped with the cooking, she stole whatever she could. If they caught her, the women yelled at her and pummeled her with their fists, so Bird Girl became clever at stealing in secret.

At night, Turak would return and demand Bird Girl's complete attention, ordering her to clean his shelter, to cook his food, and to serve his meals. Later, on his skin bedding, he would force himself on her. Bird Girl refused to cry out in her pain and humiliation, for that was what he wanted.

Yet the more Turak and his people tried to break her spirit, the stronger and more stubborn Bird Girl became. She believed that if she broke down and begged for mercy, they would be satisfied, having had their revenge, and they would kill her. Pride kept her alive.

One morning, as usual, Bird Girl was rudely awakened by Turak. Sleepily she rolled off the bedding to dress him and prepare his food. This day Bird Girl felt ill. As she stumbled across the tundra to relieve herself, she collapsed, retching on the snow. Then she felt better and sat up, wiping her mouth. Looking around, she was relieved that no one had witnessed her moment of weakness, but for the rest of the day she felt queasy.

She became sick each morning after that. Once, as she sat on the snow after vomiting, Bird Girl looked up to discover someone watching her. It was the elderly woman with whom she had spent her first night in the Ch'eekwaii camp. The two stared at each other. Then the older woman turned and walked away.

Bird Girl waited for the elder to tell the other Ch'eekwaii about her sickness, and for them to gloat over her discomfort. But this did not happen. Bird Girl noticed that the old woman, who was called Ukpik, took no interest in tormenting her, or in any of the other daily rituals of the Ch'eekwaii. Ukpik seldom spent any time with the other women, and often she chased the children away from her shelter. When the weather permitted it, the independent old woman went out alone to hunt and forage for food, returning in the evening with the meat of small animals.

Through the windy winter months, Bird Girl lost all sense of time. Each day as she stepped out of the shelter, the wind tore sharply at her face, and often the blowing snow formed a giant wall, from the sky to the ground, all around the camp.

Bird Girl dreaded the coldest days, when Turak would stay inside the shelter, restless and easily angered. Trying to keep out of his way, she hovered nervously near the walls of the dwelling, glad for the mending work that the people piled on her. If she displeased him, Turak was quick to throw her out into the cold. Then she would have to go to the homes of the other Ch'eekwaii and beg for shelter.

Many times when she found herself thrown out in the snow, Bird Girl took refuge in Ukpik's dwelling. Although the elderly woman did not invite her in, neither did she turn her away. Each time, however, Turak came looking for his slave and dragged her back to his shelter.

When the most brutal weather had passed, Turak disappeared for days, hunting over the frozen sea for seals and polar bears. Only then did Bird Girl spend a few nights in peace. During the day, the Ch'eekwaii women obeyed Turak's instructions to keep his slave busy. Bird Girl still had some slight freedom, how-ever, for the women sometimes ignored her, reluctant to give up work they enjoyed doing themselves.

One day, when Turak was gone and the wind blew hard, Bird Girl decided to air some stale clothing and blankets. As she reached up to hang a heavy fur blanket over a stick positioned between two shelters, she heard some women talking excitedly. Looking over, she saw them pointing at her.

Immediately she stopped what she was doing and watched them. When they paid so much atten-tion to her, it meant trouble.

One woman walked boldly over to her and rudely placed a hand over Bird Girl's stomach. The two stared into each other's eyes, and suddenly Bird Girl knew what the other woman suspected. The thought came like an avalanche, slowly building until it all fell crashing down into Bird Girl's mind. Her legs weak-ened, for she knew that the Ch'eekwaii woman was right. She was pregnant.

Bird Girl stumbled into Turak's shelter. Out of sight, she gasped out loud and tried to still the nausea that filled her. Her one dream . . . the hope that kept her alive in this strange land of no trees, endless skies, and angry faces . . . that dream was now threatened.

Each day as she worked outside, she had studied the landscape and had come to believe that she knew how to reach the pass through the distant mountains. She was waiting only for the right opportunity to escape.

Everything had changed in one moment. She

had thought of herself as invincible, able to jump over fallen trees, to run far without tiring, to swim against swift waters, and to hunt many animals. Now she truly had become a beaten slave, soon to cry out in the pain of giving birth to her captor's child.

Bird Girl put a hand on her belly, knowing that in a few months she would be heavy and round, unable to run. If she was to escape, it must be now.

Without further thought, she filled a pouch with dried meat and fat, a flint, a knife, and a fur blanket. It frightened her that she was stealing from Turak, but she would need these things to survive crossing the mountains.

That night the wind howled fiercely. Bird Girl forced herself from the warm shelter into the cold darkness. Trying to remember where everything was in the camp, she moved silently between familiar shelters. Dogs lifted their heads, but none barked as she walked past them and out across the frozen tundra.

When she could no longer see the Ch'eekwaii camp behind her, Bird Girl let out a long breath. The wind screeched in her face, and she leaned into it as she struggled forward, trying to keep her body pointed south toward her homeland.

She walked all that night, and the wind did not

relent. In the dawn's light the mountains seemed even farther away than she had imagined. Her legs were already tired, for she had not walked like this for a long time, and pregnancy already had begun to deplete her otherwise strong body. Bird Girl trudged through the falling snow, trying not to waste time by looking over her shoulder to see if anyone was behind her. Every now and then she stopped to rest while chewing small pieces of the meat and fat she had stolen.

When the brief daylight faded and night arrived, Bird Girl again had to rely on her inner sense of direction. In the darkness she felt the ground sloping upward and knew she had reached the hills that lay at the foot of the mountains separating the Ch'eekwaii land from that of the Gwich'in. Excitement threatened to overwhelm her, but she calmed herself. She still had a long way to go.

As the skies began to lighten, Bird Girl became exhausted. Walking made her dizzy, and her breath came in heaving gasps as she forced herself to go on. This was not the time to weaken, for death was following her.

Bird Girl could not remember how long it had taken the Ch'eekwaii hunters to reach their homeland from the caribou hunting grounds, for she had been too terrified to pay attention to the passage of time. She guessed that it had taken at least seven days. Her journey back would take longer than that, for she had no snowshoes to keep her on top of the deep snow.

Well into her fourth day, Bird Girl reached the edge of the foothills. She decided to rest before starting up the mountain slopes, because in her fatigue she was not making much progress. She looked around for shelter and saw only snowdrifts. Like a Ch'eekwaii dog, she dug a tunnel into one of them, burrowing into it with her fur blanket. Her body and mind pushed to their limits, she slept hard.

A few hours later Turak found her sleeping in the snow cave. With the eye of an expert hunter, he had easily tracked her footprints, almost hidden by a newly fallen layer of powdery snow. Now he stared down at her without compassion. She was a stubborn one. To free her would be to admit defeat in this battle between them. He could not allow that. Without further hesitation he lifted her onto his sled, turning the dogs back to Ch'eekwaii country.

Somewhere along the trail, Bird Girl awoke. When she realized where she was, deep despair overcame her. In spite of all her desperate efforts to escape, she had been recaptured.

Tears streamed down her cheeks. She thought about the life within her and wondered what would become of her and her child. She glanced back at Turak, who stood behind her on the sled. This child inside her would be part of her and part of him, two long-time enemies joined together in her womb.

Yet whenever a life is conceived, there is a sense of hope, of beginning. Bird Girl was not immune to this ageless magic as she lay on the sled, hoping for the best for the life inside her, and for herself.

## CHAPTER 12
## A child is born

*It was evening when Turak returned to the camp with Bird Girl in his sled. None of the other Ch'eekwaii came out of their shelters to greet him. Perhaps, Bird Girl thought, they feared his violent temper, knowing he was angry about having to recapture his slave.*

*Grabbing her by the arm, Turak dragged her out of the sled and into his shelter. There he pulled down her trousers and stared at her body. Throughout the camp the people were whispering that the*

Gwich'in woman was pregnant. He could not believe it. He had only taken her by force to make her suffer, never thinking about the consequences. Pressing his hand roughly against her, he felt the bulge in her belly. The thought of this Gwich'in slave carrying his child disgusted him. In a rage he lashed out, slapping her so hard that she hit the wall and fell in a heap on the ground.

Bird Girl lay there, stunned. She had hoped that the child she carried might soften his feelings toward her, but now he seemed to hate her even more. Turak pointed at her, shouting an angry stream of words, then stormed out of the shelter.

Left alone, Bird Girl felt herself losing the will to live. Even if she managed to escape to her people, they would not accept her with the Ch'eekwaii child; instead they would despise her for lying with the enemy. Nor would her child be accepted by the Ch'eekwaii, for it would be part Gwich'in.

The next day, a girl barely old enough to be a woman entered the dwelling, carrying a bowl of soup. Bird Girl eyed the girl suspiciously as she was offered the bowl. She took it and lifted it to her lips. The girl managed a nervous smile as Bird Girl drank. The broth warmed Bird Girl's empty stomach, and she savored its meaty taste. Later the girl returned with a large bundle and began to unpack. Bird Girl watched as the girl arranged her belongings, straightened Turak's bedding, and attended to other chores. What did this mean? She wondered hopefully whether, since this girl was moving in, she would be allowed to leave.

That night Turak returned. He ignored Bird Girl but occasionally acknowledged the girl, who fidgeted nervously. The girl had prepared a meal, and now Turak ate as she and Bird Girl watched.

When it was time to sleep and the girl went to Turak's bedding, Bird Girl understood. Turak had taken a new wife. For a moment Bird Girl was elated, but then she was overcome by doubts. Would the Ch'eekwaii still allow her to live? If she gave birth to her child, what would happen then? Bird Girl could not imagine them accepting the life that grew within her.

For awhile Bird Girl expected Turak to throw her out, but it did not happen. Instead, she stayed in his shelter, and at night she had to lie there as he fondled his new wife. The girl, whose name was Akpa, seemed embarrassed by the arrangement. She smiled shyly at Bird Girl when they were alone.

Life became more tolerable for Bird Girl now that Turak ignored her. But there were times during that long winter, when the sun disappeared along the monotonous horizon, leaving only a trace of pale pink light, that she held back tears, remembering her life before she was captured.

She realized that she had been arrogant, taking everything for granted and not listening to her parents' advice. She had thought herself to be strong and invulnerable, but in reality she had lived a sheltered life. Now she knew better. As she sat with her hands on the increasing bulge of her belly, Bird Girl watched the wind blowing its wall of snow across the land and sea, and the sun that peeked briefly over the edge of the sky could offer her no solace.

During those days, Akpa went everywhere with Bird Girl. When the sun lifted higher into the sky and the cold season passed, the two women spent many hours hunting for ground squirrels and spring birds returning to the land. Bird Girl found that the girl always by her side offered no true friendship, but in her loneliness she was grateful for Akpa's silent company.

The other Ch'eekwaii kept Bird Girl at a distance. Sometimes, especially when she became despondent, she thought she glimpsed compassion in their eyes. They quickly turned away; the kindness she looked for was more than they could give.

Often Bird Girl sought out Ukpik's company, only to be dragged away by an angry Turak, who did not want his Gwich'in slave to have a single friend. The elderly woman was the only one in the camp not intimidated by Turak. She disapproved of the way her people admired him and followed his example. Normally her people were just and sensible, but they had allowed Turak's hatred to corrupt them. She despised him for that. Given the chance, she welcomed the girl into her shelter and gave her food, not caring that she was the enemy. This was the old woman's way of rebelling against Turak.

Summer arrived, and Bird Girl's pregnancy was almost at an end. Her belly became so round that she could hardly walk. One day she felt a painful back cramp. The Ch'eekwaii women noticed her rubbing her back and told her that the time had come for her to give birth.

Bird Girl grew afraid. She had not listened to her mother's stories about having babies. Although she should have been taught to assist in childbirth, Bird Girl had managed to avoid this training. Now she regretted it, fearing for this child inside her.

Anxiety filled her as the pain increased along her back. Bird Girl bit her lip to fight off the pulsating cramps as the women led her to the birthing hut some distance from the camp.

Two nights passed, and Bird Girl's contractions continued. The midwives encouraged her to walk rather than sit, and she found that it helped keep her mind off the growing pain. On the third day the women tried to get her to rest, but whenever Bird Girl began to fall asleep, sharp pains awakened her. Just when she thought she could bear the pain no more, there came a tremendous urge to push.

The women held Bird Girl in a sitting position and spoke words of encouragement. She had thought the labor pains unbearable, but as she struggled to push with no strength left, she knew an even greater sense of defeat. Suddenly a burst of searing pain caught her unaware. Before she could cry out, a large baby slid into the waiting hands of the midwife, and Bird Girl felt great relief.

The women wiped off the child and wrapped him in fox skin, giving Bird Girl only a brief glimpse of her newborn son's black hair as they carried him out of the shelter. One elderly woman stayed to help

Bird Girl as her body dispelled the afterbirth, which the woman wrapped carefully in skin and took away.

Bird Girl lay back, exhausted, and fell asleep. She slept all that day and well into the night. When she awoke, she found herself alone, feeling sore but well rested. A deep sense of peace swept over her as she remembered giving birth to her child. Yearning to hold him in her arms, Bird Girl walked weakly back to the camp.

Inside Turak's dwelling she found Akpa cradling her child. A look of guilt flooded the young girl's face as Bird Girl reached for the baby. Turak's face darkened with rage. He grabbed Bird Girl roughly by the arm and dragged her out of the shelter.

Turak flung her to the ground, and she immediately rolled onto her feet. She lunged towards him, trying to fight her way back to her child, but Turak stood like a wall, tall and fearsome, in her path. She fought back fiercely, but again Turak dragged her away from the entrance. This time he shoved her down so hard that she lay there, unable to rise.

Suddenly everything became clear. They were stealing her baby. She had been led to believe that she would be allowed to live a decent life with her child. It had been a lie. Turak was not finished tormenting her.

He had told Akpa to watch her in case she tried to run away or to kill herself. He had wanted her to give birth to the child simply so he could take it away. This was his new way of making her suffer.

Enraged, Bird Girl struggled off the ground and stumbled back into Turak's shelter, screaming for revenge in her Gwich'in tongue. Turak hit her hard with his fist, and her knees buckled. Then Turak dragged her across the camp into Ukpik's dwelling.

There the two Ch'eekwaii argued loudly. Ukpik swore angrily at Turak for having abused this girl so cruelly. Turak no longer had any tolerance for disobedient women, whether a slave or an elder, and he cursed back. If Ukpik felt sorry for the girl, he said, then she could have her. Finally he stomped out of the shelter, shouting that the Gwich'in should be grateful he did not kill her.

When he was gone, Ukpik's small shoulders sagged. What would she do with the enemy girl no one wanted? They had used her and tossed her aside. She shook her head sadly, for she and this Gwich'in had much in common. Both were considered worthless — she because of her age, the girl because she was one of the enemy.

Days passed, and Ukpik discouraged Bird Girl

from leaving her dwelling. When at last Bird Girl
emerged, she found that the Ch'eekwaii ignored her,
acting as if she were not there. They seemed embarrassed by her presence, for she no longer served any
purpose. Only Turak wanted her to remain with
them, so he could use her child to torment her.

Turak would not allow Bird Girl to take any part

in her son's life. After enduring all the pain and humiliation the Ch'eekwaii had inflicted on her, Bird Girl found the knowledge that her newborn child was nearby — in Turak's dwelling, where she was forbidden to go — to be pure agony. Overcome by grief, she spent her nights weeping in great sorrow.

## CHAPTER 13
### Following a dream

For five years Daagoo watched the young boys he had trained as hunters grow into manhood and start families of their own. Yet he did not take a wife himself. Instead, Daagoo cared for his mother, Shreenyaa, as she grew older, helping her gather wood and providing her with food.

Many times Shreenyaa felt sorry for her son, remembering his carefree spirit and missing that side of him. Now he was withdrawn and serious. She wondered if he would ever smile again.

One day Daagoo took out the mooseskin map he had carried with him ever since he was a child. As he touched it gently, he knew the time had come for him to leave, to explore the land the way he had longed to for so many years. Before he could lose his courage, he told his mother about his decision.

"I have noticed that you are not happy," she said, tears glistening in her eyes. "You must do what you want, or you will never be happy."

She hugged her son, and he embraced her with silent tears.

Daagoo spent the following days preparing for his journey. The Gwich'in band did not question his plans. His dream seemed ridiculous, but out of respect they said nothing. He was relieved that he did not have to answer their questions, for his only clear plan was to follow the map to the ancient route south, leading to the Land of the Sun.

He regretted that he would not be able to say goodbye to Bird Girl's three brothers, but they were gone on one of their many long journeys into the mountains. Although years had passed, they had never given up hope of finding their sister.

When the day came for Daagoo to leave, his mother stood by her shelter and waved bravely. Others in the band simply stared, not understanding this man's restlessness. As he walked away, one of the little boys blurted out, "Where are you going?"

"I am going to follow the sun!" he answered simply, and did not look back.

Throughout the winter, Daagoo traveled far, walking easily on the frozen rivers and lakes. Following the route shown on the skin map, he pondered the words of the elder who had described it long ago.

"It is said that our people went this way," the old man had told him, drawing in the dirt a path leading south. "We do not know whether they reached the Land of the Sun, or even whether that place truly exists."

Weeks passed, then months. The land changed little along the way. Daagoo saw snow and familiar animals, but no people. Then, one day, he surprised a hunting party. For a moment they did not know how to react, and neither did Daagoo.

"Who are you?" one of them asked.

Daagoo was relieved to hear his own language, although the accent was different.

"I am Daagoo," he answered. "I come from Gwichyaa Zhee (People of the Flats)." He pointed north in the direction of his homeland.

The men came forward to shake his hands in friendship. "We know of our relatives that way," one said, inviting Daagoo to share a meal with them. "Our main camp is far from here, but we always hunt in this area for moose. So far we have not seen any."

Everyone eyed Daagoo curiously.

"Where are you traveling to?" another man asked.

Daagoo brought out the map and began to tell his story. The men stared at him. When he finished, after a long silence, one of them said, "That is a long way from here. It will take months to get there."

Daagoo nodded his head. He knew that his journey had barely begun.

"You are very curious," said one man. "I admire that. It must have been hard to leave your family."

Daagoo nodded again, pleased with the stranger's insight. He wondered if other men secretly shared his dream.

That night these Gwich'in shared their camp and their stories with Daagoo, and he learned that his people were spread farther across the land than he had guessed.

"Farther south is coastline," a man explained, "but in winter all of this land becomes cold and covered with snow. Do you really believe that there is

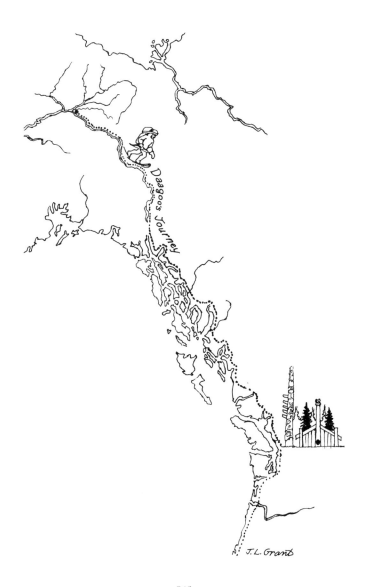

J.L. Grant

a land where the sun shines all the time?"

Daagoo said yes. He was too far from home to begin doubting the legend now.

The next morning he bid his new friends farewell. They admired his courage and were eager to tell their families about this man.

"Be careful as you go farther south," they warned him. "The people are our enemies. They speak a different language and do not welcome strangers. It will be better if you have something to trade with them. That will keep you alive."

Daagoo wished he had thought of that earlier. He should have brought some of the fine skins and furs that his mother had tanned. As he walked away, he regretted not having planned better for this trip.

Alone again as winter wore on, Daagoo found the landscape changing from flatlands to hills, then from hills to mountains. Much of his time was spent searching for passes through the many mountain ranges he encountered. He climbed over high ridges and down into deep canyons. Along the way he saw familiar animals such as lynx and bear. He considered trapping them for their fur, but decided he did not want to burden himself by carrying it.

Daagoo lost track of time as the months went by.

Gradually it became warmer, and the mountains ran with the sludge of mud mixed with melted snow. The trees became larger and thicker, and were covered with green moss. To keep himself from falling down the steep slopes, Daagoo often grabbed the stems of plants only to discover that many had sharp thorns that cut like knives. His hands became torn and bruised from climbing.

The moose disappeared, and it became difficult to find animals to hunt. But Daagoo had expected the animals to change as the land changed, so he kept himself alive on whatever small game he could find. Even the squirrels were different from those he was accustomed to eating.

It was well into spring when Daagoo spotted another group of people. They did not see him, so he followed them. They walked a long distance, swinging an animal, somewhat like a caribou but smaller, on a pole carried between two men. Daagoo stayed at a safe distance behind them, undetected, although a few of the men looked over their shoulders as if suspecting they were being followed. Finally they arrived at a camp like none Daagoo had ever seen.

It was a large settlement of wooden shelters facing the water in a single row. Colored shields

J. L. Grand

depicting strange painted faces hung high above the doors. Caches for drying fish and meat stood along the shore, and people moved about as smoke from open fires drifted in the air.

The village was along the banks of the largest river Daagoo had ever seen. It was so wide he could see no land on the other side, and he could feel its dampness in the air. Along the beaches lay many enormous wooden canoes, built large to match the great size of the water, and colorfully decorated with animal emblems.

The men put down the animal they had killed as their people gathered to welcome them home. Then the hunters pointed toward the woods where Daagoo was hiding. He shrank back, thinking he had been discovered. After a while, the crowd settled down and Daagoo relaxed too. The aroma of meat cooking filled the air, and he licked his lips hungrily.

Daagoo waited until long after the people had gone into their houses before daring to come out. He crept silently into the camp and stole the meat they had left on rocks near the campfire. Feeling a bit guilty, he returned to his hiding place to chew the tender meat. It resembled caribou but tasted sweeter, and he enjoyed it greatly.

The following morning, Daagoo sneaked back to watch the people, his curiosity stirred by their formal appearance. Unlike the Gwich'in, who wore only skins and fur, these people wore elaborate fur robes against the chill of the wind off the water. Some favored soft mantles woven from tree bark, while others had colorful, patterned capes, apparently woven from animal fur spun into fat threads. They also wore many kinds of hats, beautifully carved from wood into the shape of birds or animals, or woven from dyed grass and tree bark.

Daagoo noticed many people wearing jewelry made from the shells of sea creatures. These shells were rare treasures to his Gwich'in people, who traded many goods to their coastal neighbors for them. And these people had a strange orange metal, which they fashioned into ornaments and sharp weapons.

He spent the day watching these people and that night, when they were asleep, he crept out to steal more meat. This would be his last theft, Daagoo decided. Then he would move on.

Again he filled his skin pouch with the savory meat, and he was about to leave when he sensed he was not alone. Suddenly he was surrounded by fierce-looking men, some with rings sticking out of their noses, all carrying spears and metal daggers. Daagoo stood absolutely still with his hands in the air. He knew that one mistake might cost him his life.

The men moved cautiously toward him. Daagoo tried to smile but was too frightened. The men were frightened, too, thinking this strange figure might be a spirit from the other world.

The tallest man in the group came forward, yelling in a strange guttural language, but Daagoo did not dare answer. Then the chief reached out to touch him. When he discovered that Daagoo was human, he spoke again, more calmly. The language clicked and gulped, as if he were swallowing his words. His people nodded, relaxing and turning to stare at Daagoo.

Daagoo — once a leader, a hunter, and a scout — now stood before these people as a thief. He felt ashamed. If they punished him, it would be justified.

The chief questioned him aggressively. His eyes, dark and glistening, sent fear tingling down Daagoo's spine. When the Gwich'in reached into his pouch to bring out his map, sharp spears were thrust toward him. Daagoo quickly put his hands back in the air.

One of the spear-wielding men leaned forward, reached into the pouch, and took out the map, giving

Daagoo a forbidding look. The map was passed to the chief, who studied it carefully. Then the chief asked Daagoo a question, his voice filled with curiosity. Gingerly, Daagoo leaned over and pointed to the map, using gestures to explain where he was going. The men stood around him, trying to understand.

Finally a look of comprehension fell over the leader's face. He explained to his people about Daagoo's journey, and they all murmured in awe. Daagoo was unaware that these people were one of the most powerful and warlike clans in the whole land. Ordinarily they would have strung him up by the neck to hang until he died, or made a useful slave of him. But his story was so unusual that they could only stand and stare at this traveler from afar who was following the sun.

Much to Daagoo's surprise, the chief motioned him to sit down on a woven grass mat near the fire. The chief handed him the pouch filled with meat. Daagoo felt himself blush as he took back the bag with a nod of thanks. Someone gave him a bowl of broth, which he drank gratefully. When he finished, the chief questioned him again with words and hand gestures, and Daagoo struggled to answer.

The men stared at their visitor in disbelief, straining to understand. Why would a man endanger his life to explore an unknown place? Like the Gwich'in, these people, the Tlingits, led lives tightly interwoven with deeply held traditions. Any Tlingit man who strayed outside tradition would bring upon himself anger and contempt. But Daagoo was not a Tlingit, so his strangeness was no threat to them. Although they could not understand him, they decided to respect his dream of finding the Land of the Sun.

Daagoo remained with the Tlingits long enough to learn something about the way they lived. They filled their lives with ceremonies, art, songs, and stories, and depicted their history in the crests that decorated their hats and the frames of their doorways. To Daagoo they seemed wealthy, possessing many goods that they had traded from the Gwich'in and other peoples.

Most of their food came from the sea, and, like the Gwich'in, they loved salmon meat. In time the Tlingits took Daagoo out in their beautiful canoes, teaching him how to catch octopus and ocean fish. They also showed him how to dig for clams on the beach at low tide.

Daagoo saw many differences between these people and his own. Yet the Tlingits, like the Gwich'in, lived off the land and the water, used rituals to honor their spirits and those of the birds and animals, and held to strict traditions that tolerated no disobedience.

One morning, when he felt ready to leave, Daagoo surveyed his sparse belongings. Because he did not know what kind of people, animals, or land he would find farther south, he wanted to take some food with him, but he did not have much to trade.

Daagoo had seen how much the Tlingits loved music. He told their leader he would like to trade a song for food. The chief laughed, for it was the most unusual idea he had ever heard. Then, noticing Daagoo's seriousness, he decided to consider the offer.

The whole clan gathered to listen. Daagoo's song was short but beautiful, filled with the longing of a farewell to a loved one.

*Aiyii yi yaaa, aiyii yi yaaaaaa*
*Aiyii yi yaaa, aiyii yi yaaaaa*

*Khit ts'a neet'ihiih khyaa,*
    *yeendaa ji' chan neenahall'yaa*
(I will always love you. I will see you again.)

*Aiyii yi yaaa, aiyii yi yaaaaaa*
*Aiyii yi yaaa, aiyii yi yaaaaa*

*Shanandaii, shii chan nineehaldaii.*
(Remember me. I will always remember you.)

As he sang, Daagoo thought of his mother and father, and his voice filled with passion. Intrigued, the chief began to sing the song along with Daagoo. When they had finished, they turned to the others, who clapped in approval.

Smiling, the leader put his arms around the embarrassed Daagoo. He liked the song and would trade food for it. Daagoo promised that when he returned to his people, he would tell them that they could never again sing this song, for it now belonged to the Tlingit clan.

Later, Daagoo's new friends explained to him that along the coastline were more people who had warred among themselves for many generations, battling for land and food. They told him about the many different landscapes: desert country, hills, and ocean beaches. They, too, had legends about lands that lay far to the south.

Daagoo thanked them for their help and waved farewell. As he walked away, the Tlingits tried to imaginc the foreign places and hostile tribes he would encounter on his journey. What would become of this man and his strange quest?

## CHAPTER 14
## The Land of the Sun

*D*aagoo traveled more quickly in the months
that followed. The land became less moun-
tainous, and he grew stronger as he walked.
Following the water's edge for mile after mile, he
encountered no people, only the ruins of many
deserted villages, lying among tree branches and
pieces of splintered wood. He easily found food,
gathering mussels and clams, and catching fish
with wooden hooks the way the Tlingits had taught
him. He shed his heavy clothes because the air was

warm even after the sun went down at night.

Nine months after leaving his band in the north, Daagoo walked along a sandy beach, looking out at this serene land. The breeze blew salty air in from the sea that stretched farther than his eyes could see. Seagulls and snipes squawked around him as he left his footprints in the smooth sand. He had found the Land of the Sun.

Lying down in the sand, basking in the warm sunshine, Daagoo wondered whether he should continue his journey. Here the sun shone warmly overhead, and the sea provided him with plenty to eat. Still, Daagoo decided to move on. This was a rich country, but something even better might be ahead. The urge to see what lay beyond the horizon still possessed him.

Instead of following the route on his map, which led inland to the place where the other Gwich'in people had gone, Daagoo decided to stay near the shores of the ocean. Walking along the beach one day, he suddenly realized how far away he was from his people. There was no one to help him if he became wounded or fell into danger. If he died here, only the birds and tiny sea creatures waiting to feast on his body would care.

The old Gwich'in teaching that people need

each other to survive came into his mind. As he stood there, thousands of miles from home, this lesson had real meaning for him for the first time. Deeply feeling his complete aloneness, Daagoo decided to spend just a few more days exploring this land. Then he would return to his people.

Traveling farther south, he found more coastline, beautiful landscapes of sea and sand. The seafood he ate kept him healthy, and the brilliant sun warmed him, darkening his skin. The empty beaches became familiar to him, and each day that passed made him more reluctant to leave.

Months went by, until finally there came a day when it was too hot. Sweating and uncomfortable, Daagoo longed for the land of snow and cold, remembering his people and wondering how they were. Consulting his map, he decided that he had gone far enough. Ahead of him he could see mountains that would be difficult to cross, and he missed his people and his homeland. Admitting that his restlessness was gone, Daagoo decided to leave the next day, to return to his people and tell them about the Land of the Sun.

That night, as Daagoo lay looking up at the sky, he heard someone crying. He listened intently. The crying stopped, then started again. It sounded like a woman in pain.

Daagoo followed the noise, relying on the stars to shed light on trees and shrubs as he walked past them in the darkness. Each time the crying stopped, he waited until it began again. Finally he could tell that the woman was nearby. She must have sensed Daagoo's presence, because she became silent for a long time. Morning approached, and Daagoo napped as he quietly waited to hear her again.

Instead, he was awakened by a baby crying. Surprised at how close it sounded, he peeked out from behind a shrub and saw a young woman with flowing black hair holding a newborn child in a swathe of tanned deerskin. He wondered what to do, for obviously she had been in labor all night and had just given birth. He did not want to frighten her.

Then the woman surprised Daagoo by calling out sharply in a foreign tongue. Feeling guilty for spying on her, Daagoo stood up. The girl gasped, and he held out his hands in peace, trying to make her understand that he would not harm her. She stared at him from under long lashes, then gestured for him to sit near her.

The woman rocked the infant in her arms.

Daagoo returned her stare shyly. He had never seen a woman like her, with hair so long and glistening, and skin darkened by the sun. It felt good to see another human again.

Yet, as the woman continued to stare curiously at him, he felt himself becoming uncomfortable. The hot sun forced him to wear only a sheath of skin tied around his waist. His hair had grown long, and he kept it in tight braids. How strange he must appear to this woman.

Still looking him in the eye, she questioned him in her language. He had left the map back at his camp, so he drew a map in the sand, gesturing and speaking in his Gwich'in tongue to describe his far-away homeland. He talked about how long the journey had taken, drawing a moon and pointing to the sky, then to places on the map, then to himself, then to the place where he sat.

The woman listened carefully, her eyes opening wide. She wanted to ask more questions but knew that he would not understand her. Weary from having given birth, she motioned for Daagoo to come closer, then handed him the infant and lay down on the ground to sleep.

Daagoo was surprised to find himself caring for

the newborn. The woman awoke briefly to feed her child and slept again; it was late in the afternoon before she finally stirred. Daagoo gestured that he was leaving to find food and gave her back the child.

He walked away, tempted to keep going, but something inside him would not allow him to abandon this woman. Instead he caught a fish, returned to his camp to gather his possessions, and rejoined the woman, whom he found feeding her child.

Building a rack out of sticks and placing it over the fire, Daagoo cooked the fish as the woman watched. The two strangers ate in silence. Later, she motioned for him to sleep on the ground nearby. In the days that followed Daagoo continued to bring food for them to share. The woman smiled each time he returned.

As she regained her strength, the woman fell into the habit of cooking for him. Soon Daagoo found himself watching the infant when the woman left to forage for edible plants. She learned to call him by name, saying "Daagoo" with only a hint of accent. Daagoo, however, could not pronounce her name correctly, so he called her Sunshine in his own language.

When he was not away foraging for food and she was not busy breast-feeding her baby, Daagoo used gestures to ask Sunshine where her people were, but she would not answer. Each time he asked, she sadly looked away.

One day, waiting for Sunshine to return, Daagoo sat cuddling and talking to the baby, who cooed softly. This was a language Daagoo understood.

Then he heard a large animal approaching. He almost dropped the baby when he looked up to see Sunshine sitting high on the back of an animal that looked like a moose.

For a moment Daagoo wanted to turn and run, but curiosity made him sit still. The animal whinnied loudly and lifted its two front feet off the ground. Daagoo expected Sunshine to fall off, but she held onto the animal's mane. She smiled encouragingly, and Daagoo decided she must be a medicine woman able to control animals. He moved toward the creature, then stepped back when it snorted at him. So the woman took Daagoo by the hand, showing him how to touch the magnificent beast.

A thrill ran down Daagoo's spine as he moved his hands over its smooth brown hair. He asked questions in his language, and Sunshine answered in hers. Neither understood the other's words, but as they shared their excitement it did not matter.

Together they traveled inland on the back of the animal. There the two discovered a cave where they made a home. They hunted for deer and small animals, and Daagoo helped Sunshine tan the skins and dry the meat. He realized that he had never made a conscious decision to stay with this woman and help care for her child, yet he did not leave.

At the same time, Sunshine felt that she was helping this man from a faraway land by teaching him and hunting with him. What Daagoo was doing here she could not fully understand. Perhaps he was lost or had been forced to leave his home. She took pity on him, allowing him to stay and help with her child. They needed each other for survival.

As time passed, these two people thrown together by accident became familiar with one another. Although they still could not understand each other except by hand gestures, they hunted and foraged well together.

Daagoo spent his free time learning to ride the horse. Sunshine was a patient teacher, showing him how to get on and off, how to make it go forward or turn. Many times her face would brighten into a huge smile when Daagoo struggled to mount the animal and fell off, but she did not laugh for fear of embarrassing him.

Gradually mastering this skill, Daagoo learned to ride the horse slowly around the camp. Each morning he awoke early, determined to do better. In time he could race it along the shores of the ocean, his hair blowing back in complete freedom. When he rode the animal, Daagoo was as happy as he had ever imagined he could be.

Days passed swiftly, and before they knew it a year had gone by. Communication was still slow between them, but little by little Daagoo and Sunshine began to understand each other's languages. The infant grew into a sturdy boy, whom Daagoo called Dinjii Tsal, which meant Little Man. Sunshine accepted this name for her son, understanding that a name in her language would be hard for Daagoo to pronounce. Many times he stumbled over words that she tried to teach him.

As he grew up, Dinjii Tsal learned both languages and was able to help his mother and Daagoo talk to each other. A curious boy, Dinjii Tsal asked Daagoo many questions about his faraway homeland. As Daagoo once had struggled to imagine the Land of the Sun, Dinjii Tsal could hardly believe that a Land of Snow existed far to the north.

"Ice and snow are very cold," Daagoo said. "You have to wear animal skins and furs to keep warm. It is not like this Land of the Sun where you wear only a sheath of skin and moccasins."

Sunshine watched her son laughing and talking with Daagoo. She now understood that Daagoo had left his people simply because he wanted to find the

Land of the Sun. She could not imagine the harsh land he described as his home. How could anyone survive in a place where the warmth of summer lasted only three months? She did not think she could live in such a country.

In answer to his questions, Sunshine explained to Daagoo why he had encountered no people as he had walked south along the coastline. A few years before, a giant wave, caused by a great trembling of the earth, had destroyed the villages near the ocean. This land, in all its beauty, could be treacherous to those who lived on it, and many tribes had moved inland, preferring to live where the earth was quiet.

Sunshine also told Daagoo about her people, who lived near the coast many miles to the south. They were a strong, fiercely independent tribe with many enemies. Down through the centuries, bandits had been a constant threat to them, but her people had never surrendered.

She described how a band of the marauders had captured her, and how she had escaped in time to give birth to her son. She could never return to her tribe, for they would kill her child because it had been fathered by one of their enemies. She could not bear to lose Dinjii Tsal.

Although he had once vowed never to have a family, now Daagoo could not imagine not having one. He felt a happiness he had never known. Sunshine had been young when the bandits kidnapped her, and their brutal mistreatment had left her with a deep fear and mistrust of men. Yet time can heal such wounds, and she gradually became fond of Daagoo. He was like a father to her son, teaching him how to ride the horse and how to fish. Each night he spun tales and legends about the Land of Snow until the little boy fell into a contented sleep.

As Dinjii Tsal grew older, Daagoo and Sunshine became even closer. One night they consummated their love for each other, simply and quietly.

Months later, Sunshine told Daagoo she was expecting another child. Although she had been raised to be strong, Daagoo and Dinjii Tsal watched Sunshine carefully, not wanting her to become overtired. When the time came for her to give birth, Sunshine said she had to go out alone. Daagoo objected, but she assured him that this was the way of all women. Still, after she had gone, Daagoo and Dinjii Tsal worried about her.

Late in the evening, long after Dinjii Tsal had fallen asleep, Sunshine walked slowly back to their camp with a small bundle in her arms. Daagoo rushed forward, his knees trembling. She smiled at him and handed him the bundle, and he peeked within the folds. There he saw his son, a small red creature squirming and gnawing on its tiny knuckles. A chill tingled through Daagoo's spine, and he felt an overwhelming love for this tiny child.

Sunshine and Daagoo named their son Ch'izhin Tsal, after Daagoo's father. Dinjii Tsal was proud to be an older brother, helping to take care of the baby and teach him.

The following years were good ones for Daagoo as he watched his family grow. Sunshine gave birth to another boy, then a girl. With such a large family to feed, Daagoo worked hard to learn the ways of this land and traveled far to look for food.

One day, as Daagoo scouted for game, he spotted animal tracks that resembled those of his horse. He followed the tracks until he smelled smoke from a campfire. Tethering his own horse, he sneaked on foot toward the camp and hid behind a bush. From there Daagoo saw men whose hair and skin were dark like his, but they were dressed in finely woven fabrics and wore shoes unlike moccasins.

Daagoo hurried back to the camp to tell Sunshine

what he had seen. A look of terror crossed her face. "We must leave this place now!" she said. "These people will kill us if they find us."

That day they moved closer to the ocean, where Daagoo hoped they would be safe. Along the beach he trained his sons to catch ocean fish and gather clams. But a short while later, when Dinjii Tsal had turned ten years old, Daagoo saw more strangers in the area. He searched beyond the mountains for another place to make their home. Eventually he found a secluded area where they could find plenty of food. But as he returned to his family's camp, he trembled at the sight of a plume of black smoke lifting into the clear sky.

His heart filled with dread as he raced the horse forward. There his worst fears came true. His family lay slaughtered and scattered across the ground. So full of life hours before, Sunshine lay in a heap, smoke rising from her burned body. The children had been killed with knives, their small bodies cut apart and strewn along the beach.

Daagoo fell hard on his knees, retching on the sand from the stench of his wife's burning flesh. When he could move again, he tried to touch Sunshine's body, but it still smoldered. Looking around, Daagoo saw many horse tracks leading south, and he was overcome with rage. He would find those cowards and avenge his family.

There was no relief for Daagoo's grief as he numbly gathered wood and, building a great fire, cremated the bodies of his loved ones. Then he sat on the ground and wept.

As he mourned, his memories took him back to the time when the three Gwich'in brothers had found the belongings of their sister, Bird Girl. Now he understood their despair in discovering she had been kidnapped. Daagoo decided he did not care if the cowards who destroyed his family killed him also. Without his family, his life had no meaning.

Putting his mourning aside, he followed the horse tracks until dark, then waited for sunrise. A wind arose, blowing the sand high into the air and making it impossible to see when daylight came. The sand-storm lasted several days. When it passed, the tracks in the sand had been erased. Daagoo feared that he would never find the men who had killed his family.

As he stood wondering what to do, Daagoo heard voices, and before he could find a hiding place, he was spotted by men approaching on horseback. They drew into a circle around him, and one man boldly asked Daagoo questions in a language he did not understand. Suspecting that these men were his family's murderers, Daagoo held up his spear, prepared to do combat. The men were momentarily surprised, then began to laugh. Suddenly something fell hard against Daagoo's skull, and he saw only blackness.

When he awoke, he found himself alone, lying on his back. He could not move. His hands and feet had been tied with rawhide to pegs driven deep into the ground. He struggled to break free, but the cords cut into his wrists. His head throbbed with pain.

Daagoo regretted not listening more closely to Sunshine when she had warned him of the dangerous bandits who roamed this land, destroying anything that stood in their path. He had never known men like these. They were vicious, not caring who they murdered. Even the Ch'eekwaii killed only their enemies; these men apparently killed for pleasure. He could only wonder about them as he waited for them to return and kill him.

Hours turned into days, and there was no sign of anyone. Daagoo accepted that the bandits had left him to die of hunger and thirst. The sun which he had sought now beat mercilessly upon him.

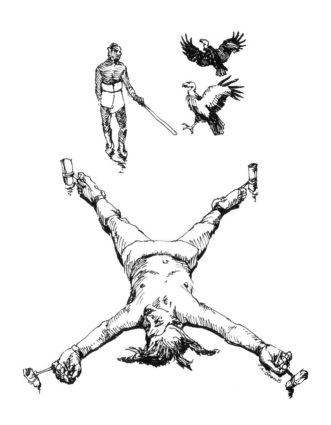

In a daze, Daagoo saw large birds hovering in the sky. He did not recognize them, but there were similar predators in the cold northland. He knew that before long the birds would begin to gnaw on his flesh. The bandits had chosen a slow, agonizing death for him.

As he slipped into delirium, many visions flitted through Daagoo's mind. He saw Sunshine running past him, smiling. Straining weakly against his bonds, he tried to chase her but she eluded him. His children played nearby, laughing and calling his name, but when he shouted for them to leave this place of bad men, they would not listen. His father looked at him in silence, and his mother cried. Then the lost sister, Bird Girl, appeared. She wept for the dead children.

Occasionally Daagoo awoke to find that nothing had changed, except that the birds now sat on the ground near him. He tried to show them he was still alive, but his body would not move. He cried out but dryness parched his tongue and his swollen throat burned with pain. Exhausted, he fell back into more senseless dreams.

Then he heard an angry voice. An old man was yelling at the birds, and the birds were screaming and squawking back. Daagoo tried to focus his eyes on the man, but his vision blurred and then he knew nothing.

## CHAPTER 15
### Revenge

*T*en *years passed after Bird Girl gave birth
to her son, the boy whom Turak and Akpa
raised, giving him the Ch'eekwaii name Kanuk.
In all those years Akpa never looked Bird Girl in
the eye. When the two met, Akpa lowered her eyes
and moved out of the way, wanting to avoid the
Gwich'in woman.*

*Turak, however, let Bird Girl know he had
not forgotten about her. He did small things to
humiliate her. Sometimes when she was eating,*

he snatched her food away and threw it to the dogs. If he saw her carrying a heavy load, he would trip her, and the other Ch'eekwaii would laugh as she fell. Never fighting back, never saying a word, Bird Girl tried to stay away from him.

Still living in Ukpik's shelter, Bird Girl worked for the elderly woman and for the few others in the camp who would allow her to come near them. With the busy old woman as her only company, Bird Girl tried to fill her days with whatever work she could find to occupy her mind and body. Yet as the seasons came and went slowly, she could not help but watch with bitterness and jealousy as her son was raised by another woman.

Kanuk grew into a sturdy boy with the strength of his mother's Gwich'in blood and the shining black hair of his Ch'eekwaii father. His brown skin glowed in a handsome face with rosy cheeks. When Bird Girl stopped to watch him run across the tundra or wrestle boldly with the other children, she remembered how free and strong she had been as a child.

Her son was the reason she did not try to escape. For years she dreamed of someday telling him that she was his true mother. Then one afternoon as she watched him play, Kanuk noticed her and stopped.

Bird Girl's heart quickened, but the boy turned and ran the other way. The longing in her eyes had frightened him.

Later, Bird Girl saw the boy's nervousness turn to scorn and revulsion. She knew then that Turak and the other Ch'eekwaii were teaching him to hate her. When he played with friends, Kanuk joined them in teasing her and throwing pebbles at her. As she turned to look at them, the children ran away, laughing.

Gradually, as the young boy grew up strong and healthy, he became like the other Ch'eekwaii children, not seeming to know or care that she existed. He was as foreign to her as Turak. Finally Bird Girl let go of her sorrow, trying to be happy that her son would enjoy a favored life with these people.

During the years that Bird Girl spent with the Ch'eekwaii, she learned much about their way of life. In the short summer months they hunted, dried fish, gathered plants and berries, and stored all the food in huge underground cellars. In autumn they moved their camp closer to the mountains, where they hunted for caribou. During the long winter the men hunted for seals, polar bears, and walruses along the sea ice. And in springtime they paddled their boats out to sea to hunt for whales.

Each year, when the whale hunters returned with their kill, a big festival took place. Ch'eekwaii came from miles around to help butcher the whale, a task that took longer than a week. Everyone became lively as men and women worked together cutting up the meat, and small children chewed muktuk, the whale skin lined with fat. Women cooked and served huge meals. Even Bird Girl felt content as everyone bustled about happily. For a very brief time, she was almost accepted by the Ch'eekwaii as she helped them cut and store the meat.

After the hard work was done, the Ch'eekwaii celebrated by dancing, singing, playing games, and laughing at each other's stories. Bird Girl watched them quietly. Sometimes she sat back, remembering her own people and the celebrations they shared. But she would not allow herself to dwell on the past, for the memories often brought her close to tears. She did not believe she could ever go back. Her people would not accept her.

Of all the games the Ch'eekwaii played, the one Bird Girl most enjoyed watching was the blanket toss. Like her people, the Ch'eekwaii played games to practice the skills they needed for hunting. The blanket toss trained them to work together in perfect unison. Strong hunters grasped the edges of a large blanket, made of walrus hides carefully sewn together, and pulled it tight. Then one agile man climbed onto the blanket and stood poised in the center. Working as one, the hunters tossed him up in the air so he could see to the far horizons. Coming down, he landed solidly on his feet, only to be tossed up again, ever higher. Great sounds of approval arose from the spectators as they watched their favorite jumpers soar high into the air. Bird Girl marveled at the sight and often had to keep herself from screaming out in excitement.

She was also fascinated by their dancing. The men would gather together and bang their hooped drums of stretched animal skins, beating an even rhythm as they chanted loudly. Bird Girl felt chills run down her spine as the men danced in perfect step, becoming one as the drums beat steadily. At no time would Bird Girl appreciate the Ch'eekwaii people more than when she watched them dance their hunting stories.

Yet it was during one whaling festival, ten years after the birth of her son, that Bird Girl came to hate the Ch'eekwaii most fiercely. In the middle of the celebrations, the men brought out a ball and began kicking it back and forth. Women and children cheered excitedly as the men played. At first it seemed an innocent game, but Bird Girl sensed that something was not right. When the ball rolled near her, she looked down to discover with horror that it was a human head.

Startled, Bird Girl looked up in time to catch a few people watching her in expectation. Standing tall among the men was Turak, looking right at her, a sneer of pleasure twisting his lips. Once more the head was kicked toward Bird Girl, coming close enough for her to recognize the face of her oldest brother.

Calling on all her inner strength, Bird Girl held back a cry of rage and despair. She refused to allow any emotion to show on her face. One of the players ran over and kicked the head back into the game, and they played on.

Just when Bird Girl had calmed herself, the Ch'eekwaii men tossed into the game the head of her second brother. This time she almost broke. "They will never see me cry!" she told herself stubbornly. She fought her grief even as the head of her third brother was kicked into play.

Bird Girl did not question how her brothers

learned that she had been kidnapped. Somehow they had come to rescue her, and the Ch'eekwaii had killed them. Her heart broke, and a single tear slid down her cheek before she could stop it.

"Why are you crying?" a Ch'eekwaii woman asked slyly.

Bird Girl replied, as lightly as she could, "Smoke from the fire is getting in my eyes." The woman and the other Ch'eekwaii nearby smiled.

As Bird Girl watched her brothers' mutilated heads being kicked back and forth, something within her snapped. Throughout all her pain, one part of her had always held on to hope. Now that part was torn in two, and she could almost feel the horrible power within her.

The light faded. The Ch'eekwaii lost interest in their game and began to wander away, but Bird Girl did not move. Quietly she sat by the campfire that had flickered out.

She thought of all that the Ch'eekwaii had done to her — the kidnapping, the rape, the beatings, the humiliation. She could have forgiven them for all of it, for slaves were always treated brutally by their captors. She understood that. She could even have forgiven them for taking away her chance to love her child, because they had loved him instead. But to kill her brothers, then flaunt it in front of her, was the ultimate insult. She would rather die than forgive them for this.

That evening she was expected to clean up after the celebration. The people all but forgot about her as they tiredly made their way to their dwellings to sleep. When all was quiet, Bird Girl walked through the camp as if in a trance, collecting the skin and fur clothing hung on racks to dry. She did not allow herself to think. Instead she felt the hatred flow through her, indulging in it as she moved from shelter to shelter, stuffing the pieces of clothing into the air holes of each one.

Almost without thought she passed by Ukpik's shelter, leaving it untouched, and headed for the dwelling where Akpa, Kanuk, and Turak lay sleeping. All the rage that she had held back for so long came flooding into her as she packed the rest of the stuffing into the holes that gave Turak's shelter air and light.

When she was done, Bird Girl returned to Ukpik's dwelling and quietly went inside. For a moment she looked down at the elderly woman lying on her bedding, looking pale and fragile as she slept soundly. Then Bird Girl went to her own bedding and took

out the hidden skin bag that she had packed in secret long ago, dreaming of escape. Putting the bag over her shoulder, she left the shelter and walked away from the Ch'eekwaii camp. She did not look back. Instead she tried to remember what awaited her on the other side of the distant mountains.

## CHAPTER 16
## A long journey home

When Daagoo awoke, he found himself lying in a cave, his body stiff and sore. He tried to remember who had rescued him. Whoever it was, they must be nearby, for they had left some meat cooking on their campfire. But Daagoo saw no one. He crawled to the fire and ate small bites of the meat. Then he collapsed on the floor of the cave, his strength gone.

That evening, while Daagoo slept, the old man returned. He sparked up his fire, warmed the cooked meat, and ate it. Staring at Daagoo, he wondered who he was and what tribe he belonged to. The old man hoped that his visitor would not become violent when he awoke. He had seen much suffering in his long life, for bandits had been a constant threat to his people. Now, in his old age, he simply longed for peace.

When Daagoo woke up late that night, he found the old man asleep. By the light of the fire's embers, Daagoo stared at the weather-beaten face of his rescuer. Then the elder stirred in his sleep and opened his eyes.

"So, you are awake," the old man said in Sunshine's language. "I thought you would surely go to the other world."

"My name is Daagoo," he replied in the same tongue.

The old man's eyes opened wide in surprise. "You are one of us?" he asked.

"I am from far away. My wife was from your tribe," Daagoo answered. Pain etched its way across his features as he struggled to sit up. He slowly told his story, trying to say the difficult words correctly.

"She was kidnapped years ago by bandits. After she escaped from them, she gave birth to a son. She did not return to her people for fear they would not accept her child. I stayed with her, and we had children of our own. But bandits murdered them all."

The old man was saddened by Daagoo's tale. "I knew this woman," he said. "She was just a girl when they took her. We searched everywhere but could not find her. I am glad to know she shared happiness with you. I will tell her people, and they will finally put her memory to rest."

In the days that followed, Daagoo gradually regained his strength. A few gashes were left on his face and hands where the birds had torn at his flesh, but the old man treated them with a salve, mixed from medicinal plants, that helped to close the wounds and ease the pain.

Yet some wounds could not be healed so easily. Bitter memories still tormented Daagoo, and he talked about his sorrow with the old man.

"What will you do now?" the elder asked one day as Daagoo watched him hang fish over the fire to dry.

Revenge filled Daagoo's mind. "I will kill those men," he insisted.

The old man looked at Daagoo for a long time. "It is no use to avenge your family," he said. "They are safe in the other world. If you go after those men again, this time they will kill you."

Daagoo did not answer.

"Go home to your people," the old man pleaded. "You have found the sun and known happiness, but now you are empty. You must go back to your own land and fill yourself again. Go back to those who love you. Your mother must be waiting for you."

Still Daagoo said nothing. The old man did not argue further, for he knew the younger man would make his own decision. When the old man grew tired of hunting alone and decided to return to his people, he invited Daagoo to go with him. Daagoo refused.

"I hope you have left behind your foolish desire for revenge," the old man said. "You are a good man. Either come join my people or go back to where you came from. Do not allow these bad memories to destroy you."

"I will move on," Daagoo said vaguely. He needed time alone to decide what to do.

The old man had found Sunshine's horse and now returned it to Daagoo, laden with meat. Bidding his friend farewell, Daagoo turned and headed north. He retraced his steps, visiting for one last time the place where he had cremated his family. Then, before he lost the courage to go on, he turned back along the path of time, toward his homeland.

The weeks turned into months as Daagoo rode the horse northward. When the weather began to cool, they headed into the mountains. One morning the animal slipped on a loose stone and fell, sending both horse and rider rolling down a rocky slope. Daagoo grabbed a handful of willows growing out of the hillside, but the horse tumbled all the way to the bottom. Slowly Daagoo made his way down to where the animal lay, two of its legs broken.

Daagoo looked at the horse sadly. This was the animal Sunshine had taught him to ride. Killing it would mean leaving behind the last trace of her. But Daagoo could see that the horse was suffering greatly, so he took out his knife and, with one quick slice through the vital veins in its neck, ended its life.

The loss of the horse saddened him, but Daagoo could only continue his journey. After several months of walking, he came upon a group of people and recognized them as the Tlingits, the proud people to whom he had once traded a song for food.

Daagoo hesitated, unsure how to approach them. Would they remember him? Already armed men had surrounded him. Daagoo held up his hands and his skin map in a gesture of surrender. One of the men spoke to the others, and they smiled. They remembered

Daagoo, the traveler who had gone south following the sun.

The men took him back to their village, where their new chief greeted him as an old friend. Many Tlingits invited Daagoo into their homes and shared their food with him, eager to hear his stories. Daagoo still did not understand the Tlingit language, but using hand gestures and Gwich'in words he managed to convey all that had happened to him. He told them about riding the horse, about looking out over the great ocean, and about walking on beaches of sand hot from the sun. The people listened, amazed by his adventures.

While Daagoo stayed with them, he hunted deer, tanned the skins, and made warm clothing for himself. Winter was approaching and he needed to move on. He figured that by the time he found his way north, the lakes would be frozen hard enough to cross. Once more Daagoo waved goodbye to the people who had helped him. He would never see them again, but they would live in his memory, and he would live in their legends.

Daagoo arrived in Gwich'in territory in late autumn. He expected to encounter hunters along the trails but saw no one. Killing a moose, he paused to dry the meat, tanning some of its hide and cutting the rest into strips of rawhide, which he would use later to make snowshoes. The rivers were not yet frozen, and Daagoo considered stopping to build a canoe to speed his journey. Instead he walked along the familiar banks of the Yuukon. The fall colors were drifting from gold into brown, and Daagoo knew it would not be long before the first snow.

He watched the seasons change, leaves being blown off the trees even as the snow fell. Then came the bitter cold, when the ice along the edges of the river expanded and froze harder. Although he had grown soft in the warm country, Daagoo was determined not to let this defeat him. In time he would adapt to this land again. The snowshoes he had constructed were not as strong as those his father had once made, but they were good enough to keep him on top of the deepening snow.

At last, as he neared one of his people's traditional winter campsites, Daagoo recognized signs of human life. Suddenly he wondered whether it had been a mistake to return. Was his mother still alive? Had everyone forgotten him? Should he have stayed in the Land of the Sun? He felt like a foreigner in this world in which he had been born. Perhaps his long journey had been for nothing. Memories of Sunshine and their children still tormented him, and the grief he felt over their deaths caused him to doubt whether anything would truly matter to him ever again.

# CHAPTER 17
## Reunion

A s he approached the Gwich'in camp, Daagoo remembered his mother's words from long ago.

"We have to trust in our future," she had said. All the women whose husbands and sons had been murdered agreed with her, knowing that without trust they could not move ahead.

"I have to trust in my future," Daagoo told himself now.

The Gwich'in people, always alert to danger, quickly spotted him coming toward their camp.

Strong men stepped forward protectively while children and women peeked out at him from inside their caribou skin shelters. Daagoo's eyes searched for a familiar face, but he did not find one.

"Stop there!" the chief commanded, and Daagoo froze. "Who are you and what do you want?"

"I am Daagoo," he said hesitantly. It felt strange to speak his own language again. "I was born in this land. Many years ago I left to seek the Land of the Sun."

The Gwich'in men gathered together to speak privately. Then their chief came forward. "Come into my shelter and tell me about yourself," he said.

All eyes were upon Daagoo as he made his way into the tent, feeling like a stranger from another world. They sat down, and the chief handed Daagoo a bowl of fish broth, a courtesy most Gwich'in offered their visitors. "You say that you left this land to journey to the Land of the Sun?"

Daagoo took the bowl as he nodded his head. After drinking the broth, Daagoo filled the silence by telling these men of his long journey. They were spellbound by his description of faraway tribes, of powerful animals that carried people on their backs, of a land with no snow where the sun shone all year long, and of a river so wide that no land could be seen on the other side.

When Daagoo had finished, the men stared at him. Their leader spoke. "We have heard of you. No one believed you would ever return."

Daagoo asked if this was the same band he had left behind.

"No, we are not," the chief answered, "but many of our people joined this band from other bands. Why do you ask?"

"When I went away, I left my mother behind, with the rest of the band. I do not know if she is still alive," Daagoo said.

Daagoo told the chief his mother's name, but the man did not remember her. "Look around and see if you can find anyone you know," he suggested.

That night Daagoo slept in the chief's tent, and in the morning he introduced himself to the rest of the band. Friendly and curious about him, they were eager to talk to Daagoo, but he did not recognize any of them. No one could tell him about the people he had left behind.

Although it was clear that these were not Daagoo's people, their leader, whose name was Vasdik, invited Daagoo to stay with the band for the winter. Daagoo accepted the offer gratefully, knowing that the cold weather was moving in quickly and it would be hard to survive on his own. He spent the winter recalling nearly forgotten skills and learning again the ways of his harsh homeland. Many times Daagoo thought longingly of the Land of the Sun, where he had easily lived on fish and clams. Now he had to travel far in search of game.

Each evening, after their meal, the people questioned Daagoo about his life in the Land of the Sun. Again and again they wanted to hear about the sand, the warm sun, the woman and his children, the bandits, and the horse. They loved to imagine themselves riding a strong, graceful animal as it ran long distances.

As Daagoo shared his stories, especially the ones about Sunshine and their children, his heart slowly healed. At times he laughed heartily at the stories told by the other men.

Vasdik was glad to have him in his band, for Daagoo proved to be a good hunter, sometimes catching a brace of spruce grouse, other times a pair of rabbits. Usually it was a mistake to accept a loner into a band, for the loner often turned out to be lazy, which was why his own people had banished him.

But Daagoo was a hardworking loner and earned the respect of everyone in the camp.

One day, while visiting Vasdik and his family, Daagoo heard the chief's wife ask one of her sons to take some furs downriver to be tanned by the crazy woman.

"Who is this crazy woman?" Daagoo asked.

"She is the woman who lived with the Ch'eekwaii," the wife replied shyly.

Daagoo stood up, excited. "What is her name?" he asked.

The chief and his wife both shrugged.

"Everyone calls her Crazy Woman," Vasdik said. "We took her in several years ago. An old couple in our band found her peeking out at them from the brush, using birdcalls to get their attention. Curious, they coaxed her out of hiding. When they heard her story, they took pity on her, allowing her to live in their shelter in secret.

"My father, who was our band's chief then, heard the children talking about a strange woman living with the elders. He found her in their tent and persuaded her to tell him her story."

"What had happened to her?" Daagoo asked.

"She said she had been kidnapped by the

Ch'eekwaii and kept as a slave for many years," Vasdik answered. "When her brothers came to rescue her, the Ch'eekwaii murdered them. In revenge the woman killed all the Ch'eekwaii by smothering them with smoke in their shelters."

The chief continued. "After telling us her story, she left to search for her parents, whom she believed to be alive. She was gone for many weeks, and when she returned she said nothing. Since then she has kept to herself.

"Now she lives down the river from us. We give her our help when she needs it, but most of the time she trails behind us and takes care of herself. She is skilled in the ways of the land."

Daagoo said he wanted to meet this woman.

"You can try, but she does not like people to bother her," the chief said. "Sometimes, when we approach her, she yells at us to go away. That is why we call her Crazy Woman. She spends too much time alone."

Daagoo nodded. "I will be careful. She sounds like someone I once knew."

The leader watched Daagoo leave the shelter, feeling sorry for this man who had lost not only his family in the Land of the Sun but also his own Gwich'in people. No doubt he would spend the rest of his life searching for his loved ones.

Hurrying to his tent, Daagoo dressed warmly and filled a bag with marten fur as a small gift for the woman. He walked for several hours to reach her campsite, many miles down the river. From a distance he saw smoke drifting up from her skin tent. As he drew nearer, the woman came out of her shelter. Even from far away she had heard him approaching.

"What do you want?" she demanded.

He looked at her carefully. Although many years had passed, she still looked much the same as he remembered.

"Bird Girl, I am Daagoo," he said. "I know your name because we met years ago, when I was a young boy."

"I was called Bird Girl long ago by my father," she replied in a low, husky voice. "Now I am called Jutthunvaa', as my mother first named me."

Then the woman stood silently. Daagoo waited. Just when he thought she might chase him away, she motioned for him to come closer.

Jutthunvaa' stared at this man, studying him. She tried to remember the serious boy she had once met, to see him behind this face with its dark skin and deep lines around its mouth.

"So, you are that foolish young boy who wanted to explore rather than stay home and help his family?" she said in the same direct way that Daagoo remembered from long ago.

He recalled how, at their first meeting, he had been intrigued by the strange girl who hunted like a man. Now she was older but still strikingly lovely. Looking into her bold eyes, he saw no sign that she was crazy. Instead, the eyes that stared back at him were clear, alive with curiosity and a little humor.

Jutthunvaa' grew uncomfortable under Daagoo's staring eyes, remembering what the members of the band said about her.

"Why are you staring at me?" she demanded. "Did they tell you I was crazy?"

Daagoo nodded ever so slightly, not wanting to admit it.

Jutthunvaa' threw back her head and laughed heartily. "Ever since I was a little girl, people have thought of me as strange," she said. "I choose to live how I want, and they call me Crazy Woman. I am used to it."

Then she said, "Tell me your story. Where have you been all these years? Your mother thought you were dead."

"You know my mother?" Daagoo asked, surprised.

"Come inside my shelter," she said. "We have much to talk about."

It was unusual for a woman to speak so boldly to a man, but Daagoo now understood those who were different. He followed Jutthunvaa' into her spacious shelter, where furs, skins, and sewing implements were strewn about. She cleared a spot for him to sit down, then offered him a birch bark bowl filled with moose meat broth.

"You have seen my mother?" he asked again.

"Yes," she said. "When I returned from the Ch'eekwaii, I was adopted by this band, but I left to search for my family. I found my band and learned how they had taken in your people, but I did not find my parents.

"My people were surprised to see me alive. I spent some time with them, and eventually I met your mother. It was she who took me aside and told me the sad news about my parents' deaths.

"She said that my brothers spent years searching for me. When they failed to return from a long journey, my parents lost hope of seeing any of their children again. They became sad, so sad that my mother became ill and died. One winter day my father walked out into the cold and dark by himself. The people knew he was taking his life and did not follow him."

Jutthunvaa' paused for a moment, remembering the despair she had felt at finding out she was alone in the world.

"Your mother took me in, and we became friends. At first the band had seemed happy that I was alive, but later it was as if I were one of the Ch'eekwaii. They asked me too many questions about how I managed to stay alive when my brothers were killed. After a while, I realized that they would never trust me, so I decided to leave.

"Your mother was unhappy about it, but she could see how the people were treating me. I wanted her to come with me, but she said her life was with her people. That was the last time I saw her."

"Do you think that band is somewhere nearby?" Daagoo asked.

Jutthunvaa' eyed him thoughtfully. "You will have to find out for yourself," she said.

That afternoon Daagoo and Jutthunvaa' traded their stories. Jutthunvaa' had never spoken the whole truth about her years in captivity, but now, her memories awakened by this face from her past, she found herself telling Daagoo everything.

"As you know, I was taken by the Ch'eekwaii," she began simply. "The man who captured me used me as a slave and tried everything in his power to hurt me. I remained strong even when I bore his child, and when he stole my son and turned him against me."

Her voice broke slightly. Tears filled her eyes as the face of her long dead son came unbidden into her mind. She was silent, struggling to control her emotions. Then she began again, speaking more slowly. Daagoo had to strain to hear her words.

"Many things happened to me in the hands of that man, but I was strong. I never cried. I would not allow him to see how much he hurt me.

"After many years, my brothers finally found the village in which I lived, and they tried to rescue me. The Ch'eekwaii killed them, cutting off their heads to kick back and forth in front of me, like a game of ball."

Daagoo listened quietly. His heart filled with pity as he thought of the young girl he had met, who had been so confident about life, being treated so cruelly. Jutthunvaa' went on.

"After that, I lost all my good sense and became

like the man who held me captive. I was so filled with hatred that I killed them all, even my own son. The only one I left alive was the old woman who was kind to me."

Jutthunvaa' suddenly felt very tired, as if she had not slept for a long time. "To this day I do not know how I feel about the death of my son. I have kept it inside for so long that it does not even seem real to me anymore. All I know is that it is good to be alive for each day that passes by."

Daagoo nodded, understanding. Then he began to tell Jutthunvaa' about his life. She listened as he told about losing his wife and children, and about the murder of his father.

"I never cried for my father properly," he said softly. "Everything happened so fast, and I did not have a chance. Now when I think of him I allow myself to remember only the good memories."

The two talked late into the night, discovering it was easy to share their secrets. By the time Daagoo left Jutthunvaa's shelter to return to camp, they felt like old friends.

Throughout the winter Daagoo returned time and time again to Jutthunvaa's campsite. This did not go unnoticed, and one day Vasdik asked Daagoo, "Are you interested in taking this woman for a wife?"

Daagoo blushed. "No, it is not like that." He explained that he and Jutthunvaa' had known each other long ago and that they had much in common. He told the chief that she was not crazy at all.

"I am surprised," admitted Vasdik, who had never spoken to the woman himself. He had simply believed what everyone said about her. "Should I tell her to come and stay with us?"

"You will have to ask her," Daagoo answered. "She is independent and will make up her own mind."

"And what will you do now?" asked Vasdik.

Daagoo knew that he could no longer keep his plans secret from the chief, who had come to know him well. "In the spring I will look for my mother," he replied.

The leader nodded, then warned, "It is possible she might not still be alive."

"I have thought of that. I am prepared," Daagoo said.

Springtime arrived, and Daagoo waved farewell to the band. Among them stood Jutthunvaa'. With Daagoo's encouragement, she had joined the band, becoming respected by all in the camp. Looking back at her as he walked away, Daagoo wondered if this would always be his fate, to leave behind the people he cared about.

He traveled through the arctic lands as the sun rose higher in the sky each day. Winds from the north sometimes blew bitterly cold, but as he weathered the storms, Daagoo no longer wondered about the sun or the wind or what lay in the directions from which they came. Those questions had been put to rest by his years of exploring.

The wind, the sun, and the stars existed as far away as the mind could wander, he knew. It was his curiosity that had taken him far from his homeland, but Daagoo did not feel that he had gained any great wisdom on his long journey. Instead he thought only of the precious life he had found and lost in the Land of the Sun. Now his only hope was that his mother was still alive and he could care for her as his restless heart would not allow him to do years before.

As he walked, he considered the strangeness of his life. So long ago his father had tried to teach him that for people to survive they had to work together. That was the Gwich'in way. He had walked away from that lesson to seek his own dreams, and he had found them, yet in the end he had lost everything. He had traveled many years and thousands of miles to

find himself back where he had started, in the home-land he had abandoned, searching for the family he had left behind. Daagoo looked up into the clear blue sky and wished that somehow he could tell his father that he finally understood the ways of his people.

Now Daagoo could enjoy the beauty of his own land, content to travel its ancient trails once more. For weeks he followed the endless paths from one hunt-ing ground to another, but he saw no sign of his people. As summer approached, he realized that he needed to begin gathering supplies for winter, so he traveled up the Yuukon to the place where it con-nected with the small river flowing down from the caribou country.

There Daagoo rejoined the band with whom he had spent the previous winter. It was the month when the sun was highest, a busy time for the Gwich'in. Men and women built fishtraps and canoes, while older children kept the younger ones quiet and occupied with games. Everyone helped catch and dry the many salmon that swam up the wide river. Then, at night, they ate and rested, wearing bear grease and clothing with tassels to protect them from the mosquitoes that arrived in swarms, trying to pinch blood from them and their heavily swathed babies.

Early one morning, as Daagoo slept in his shelter, he was awakened by sounds of activity outside. Coming out, he saw that the band had visitors. A large group of people sat around the campfire, talking with Vasdik. Sometimes bands met during the summer to trade stories or goods acquired from faraway tribes. These people seemed friendly, Daagoo thought as he watched them. Many of the visitors were women and children, who sat back eating while the men talked.

Daagoo noticed that the newcomers kept glancing at him. Although he could not hear their conversation,

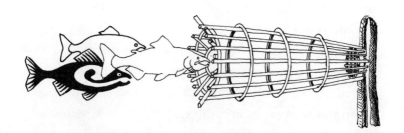

he felt sure they were talking about him. Vasdik, he realized, was telling the story of his journey to the Land of the Sun, and it was causing a great stir among the visitors. At last the chief stood up and called to Daagoo.

He rose slowly, not knowing what to expect. A shriek came from the crowd, and Daagoo saw a tall, elderly woman standing up with her arms outstretched.

He stared at the woman for a long moment before he recognized her.

"Mother?" he said, his knees growing weak.

Shreenyaa hurried through the crowd and threw her arms around him. Daagoo was stunned, for he had almost given up hope of finding her. Now he lifted his mother off the ground and hugged her.

The other visitors crowded around Daagoo eagerly. The young boys whom he had taught to hunt were grown men now, with many children; the women who had been young widows back then were now grandmothers. Daagoo smiled at how their lives had changed. He, too, had changed.

Later that day, the two bands shared their happiness with a festive celebration. As the excitement began to die down, the guests noticed Jutthunvaa' watching them. Vasdik told them her story. Then the visitors remembered how they had rejected this woman, first because she would not marry, then years later because she had lived among the Ch'eekwaii. Many were embarrassed about the way they had treated her. Jutthunvaa' would not speak to most of the visitors, for her memories of them were too painful. However, she was glad to see Daagoo's mother and greeted her warmly.

Remembering how Daagoo had once taught him to hunt, the chief of the visiting band asked Daagoo to rejoin his people. Daagoo considered the offer. When he had lived in the Land of the Sun, he had been able to survive on his own, but now, in this Land of Snow, he would need the help of other people. He would have to choose one band or the other before they went their separate ways.

"What would your decision be, Mother?" he asked.

Shreenyaa did not hesitate. "Do you remember the time when I and the rest of the band helped you make a decision about our future?" she asked. "I did that because you were young and had never made such decisions. Now you stand before me, a full-grown man, and you ask me what to do?

"If a grizzly bear stood before you, ready to kill

you, would you ask me what you should do? No, you would know what to do. You would choose to fight him and survive. That is how all your decisions should be made — by looking into your heart, into your mind, and not by listening to what everyone else says. This is your life. I will go with you, no matter which band you choose."

Daagoo smiled at his mother. Like his father, she had always given him freedom and words filled with wisdom. "I must make myself worthy of my parents someday," he said to himself.

The next morning, when his band was ready to leave, the visiting chief approached Daagoo.

"My teacher, we need to move on. Will you come with us?" he asked.

Daagoo said no, but the chief understood.

"We will see you again," he told Daagoo confidently.

Before they left, all the visitors gathered around Daagoo to wish him well. As Daagoo watched them go, he put his arm around his mother's shoulders. Then he turned and looked beyond his tent to see Jutthunvaa' watching them. Smiling, he held out his other hand to her. Jutthunvaa' hesitated. Then she, too, came to him.

Together Daagoo, his mother, and Jutthunvaa' stood watching the people from their past move on. It was the past that they would leave behind as they moved ahead into the future.

# Author's Afterword

The story you have just read is based on two legends that my mother told me long ago. I find that I am attracted to stories about people who stray from the "normal." Maybe this reflects my true nature, because I never forgot the story of Jutthunvaa' and her trials.

My biggest worry in writing her story was the violence. Although I invented the murder of Daagoo's wife and children to give him a good reason to return to his Gwich'in people, the violence in Jutthunvaa's story was a vital part of the original legend. In the end she really did kill her captors. The challenge for me was to make her motives — and those of her captors — believable.

When first writing Jutthunvaa's story, I tended to be biased against her abductor because I had been raised on hate stories about the Eskimos. I had to shed some of the prejudice that I had been taught as a child. In redrafting the story, I tried to make the Ch'eekwaii a little more humane.

Later, I had misgivings about the murders that Jutthunvaa' commits. I suddenly wanted to be politically correct and to write that Jutthunvaa', despite her suffering, walked away without hatred, taking no revenge. But the politically correct version did not ring true to heart. How could a woman who had been abused and raped, and whose brothers had been murdered, forgive so easily? In the end I decided to remain true to the legend.

Daagoo's story . . . well, that legend was truly vague. My mother said the man followed the sun, encountered foreign tribes and discovered horses in the Land of the Sun, then returned to his people years later. I had to fill a lot of blank spaces in that story.

One important addition was Daagoo's wife. I wanted to make her a Yaqui woman from the region that became Mexico and California. The Yaqui reminded me of the people along Alaska's coasts because of the way they suffered from outside invasions and survived. I admire their tenacity. But because I did not want to go into great detail about other cultures and end up with a thick novel, I only alluded to her heritage.

The idea of trading a song came from someone I met while chaperoning a group of local Native artisans to the Smithsonian Arts Festival in Washington, D.C., in 1982. This Tlingit man told me that his people owned a song that had been traded to them by the Gwich'in. He did not know how or why the song was traded, only that the song could not be sung by my people again. Once a song or dance is traded, it becomes the sole property of the clan that acquired it. Later, I could not resist adding this story to the account of Daagoo's journey through Tlingit country. The song he sings is one that we used to sing as children.

Early on, I decided not to introduce any Native people other than the Tlingits on Daagoo's journey. All Native people of America were suspicious of one another and protective of their territory, so Daagoo would not have been lucky enough to survive if he had met all the people living along the Pacific Coast. So I made him into a kind of Robinson Crusoe, leaving his footprints on a long line of sandy, un-touched beaches.

Perhaps this sounds as if the Native people of those times were constantly killing each other. It was not always like that. The Inupiat and the Athabaskans, for example, were able to relate to one another through a trading system which included other tribes through-out Alaska. It is true that the Inupiat and the Athabaskans were enemies because of things that they had done to one another over the years, but as children what made us dislike the Eskimos was the stories our elders told us.

While this story may stir up some of those memories, my hope is not to reopen a wound that has long been closed. Rather, I wished to tell a story about two young people, born long before their time, who strayed from deeply held customs. The point of the story is that we all leave home for different reasons, but one day we must come home again. That is true for almost everyone.

Velma Wallis

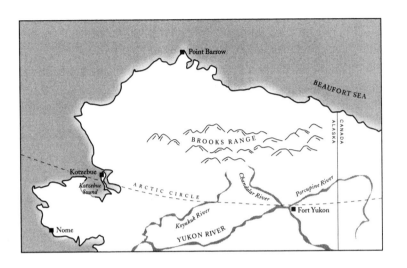

## About the
## Gwich'in and Inupiat peoples

Today the Gwich'in Athabaskans, described by Velma Wallis in this story, live in eastern Alaska and western Canada, along the Yukon, Porcupine, and Tanana Rivers. However, anthropologists believe that at one time the Gwich'in people occupied lands to the north, in the Brooks Range and in the flats and valleys of the Upper Koyukuk River, and possibly farther west toward Kotzebue Sound.

Searching for answers about why the Gwich'in

moved south, anthropologists are turning to Native Alaskan oral traditions, which describe past strained relations between the Gwich'in and the Inupiat — the north Alaska Eskimos whom the Gwich'in called the Ch'eekwaii. Scholars continue to explore the suggestion that encroachment by the Inupiat on traditionally Gwich'in lands caused violence, especially in the form of raids, which resulted in the depopulation of both groups. Because of such conflicts, the Gwich'in people may have migrated out of the "battle zone," heading east and south.

Several Athabaskan stories describe entire villages, either of Athabaskans or of Inupiat, being destroyed in surprise attacks by their enemies at night, often as acts of revenge. The assailant would plug the smoke hole of the semi-subterranean dwelling, then set fire to the structure while the occupants were asleep. These fires, fueled with birch bark or moss and stoked with animal oils such as whale oil or bear grease, would suffocate the victims before igniting into flames. A well-documented account of one such attack is found in the journal of surgeon Edward Adams (1851, unpublished manuscript, Scott Polar Institute, Cambridge, England).

Such stories form the basis for the events in *Bird*

*Girl and the Man who Followed the Sun.* Told to children at a young age, these stories served to reinforce in the culture the deep-rooted fear of chance encounters between the Gwich'in and the Inupiat. The danger of violence made necessary a network of alliances between various Native groups, which protected members when they traveled through neighboring lands. Through these alliances, a band of Gwich'in could survive even the loss of its most productive members, its hunters — as takes place in the story of Daagoo's band.

As scholars move toward recognizing the value of the oral tradition, seeking to understand the context of these parables, the writing of Velma Wallis provides a window through which readers can experience the ways of life of the early indigenous people who occupied Alaska in times past.

Miranda Wright

*Miranda Wright, an anthropologist, directs the Doyon Foundation's cultural heritage and educational programs for the Athabaskan people of Interior Alaska.*

*Author Velma Wallis with her two*
*children, Daagoo and Laura Brianna*

## About Velma Wallis

Velma Wallis was born in 1960 in Fort Yukon, a remote village of about 650 people in Interior Alaska. Growing up in a traditional Athabaskan family, Wallis was one of thirteen children. When she was thirteen, her father died and she left school to help her mother raise her younger siblings.

Wallis later moved to her father's trapping cabin, a twelve-mile walk from the village. She lived alone there intermittently for a dozen years, learning traditional skills of hunting and trapping. An avid reader, she passed her high school equivalency exam and began her first literary project — writing down a legend her mother had told her, about two abandoned old women and their struggle to survive.

That story became her first book, *Two Old Women*, published by Epicenter Press in 1993. As her second book, *Bird Girl and the Man who Followed the Sun*, went to press, Wallis was living in Fort Yukon with her husband, Jeffrey John, and their two children. The family also spends time in the neighboring village of Venetie.

## About Jim Grant

An Athabaskan Native born in 1946 in the village of Tanana, Alaska, James L. Grant Sr. was adopted and raised James G. Schrock in Southern California. Drafted into the U.S. Army in 1967, he was stationed in Europe, where he studied the masters. Later he attended Chaffey Junior College in Alta Loma, California, then returned to Alaska to study the Native Arts at the University of Alaska Fairbanks. Besides pen and ink drawings, his art includes sculpture, mask making, and oil painting. He currently lives in Fairbanks, Alaska.